THE BIBLE SELLER

R. Allen Chappell

Dedication

This series is dedicated to those Diné who still follow the Beauty Way—and while their numbers are fewer each year—they remain the well from which the people draw strength and feed the *Hozo* that binds them together.

Acknowledgments

Again, many sincere thanks to those Navajo friends and classmates who provided "grist for the mill." Their insight into Navajo thought and reservation life helped fuel a lifelong interest in the culture, one I once only observed from the other side of the fence.

Author's Note

In the back pages, you will find a small glossary of Navajo words and terms used in this story, the spelling of which may vary, somewhat, depending on which expert's opinion is referenced.

Table of Contents

1

The Mistake

In his last few moments on earth, it was only natural that Benny Klee, now in his seventy-eighth year, should blame his truck for this final dilemma.

Benny considered himself an excellent driver despite not learning the skill until quite late in life. A frugal man who scratched out a thin living as a silversmith, he managed to purchase the used truck by way of a small down payment followed by the usual monthly installments. The car dealer proved to be surprisingly honest, not only in his representation of the vehicle, but also in the arithmetic involved in the loan. Located just outside Farmington on Highway 64, the car lot was first to catch the eye of anyone coming from the reservation. The dealer, understanding what it takes to stay on the *Dinés'* good side, could even speak a smattering of the language. Benny Klee took to him at once, made his payments mostly on time, and eventually paid the truck off. Over the years, the old man maintained the vehicle as well as possible considering his meager circumstances. The wear and tear of reservation roads, however, ultimately took their toll. It was time, the old man declared, for a newer truck.

On his way in from Teec Nos Pos, in a pre-dawn drizzle, Benny was in search of a trade, a big decision for the old *Diné*, and one he didn't take lightly. Older Navajo consider any sort of trade a form of recreation; they may take days to finalize a deal on a horse or truck or even an item of old-pawn jewelry. There was no doubt in Benny's mind where he would take his business. The car dealer was still in the same location, proof enough for Benny Klee of the man's ongoing dedication to a square deal. Benny, being unaware at the time, that this current truck would, unfortunately, be his last.

In the first gray light of dawn the old man crossed the New Mexico state line—the sage flats unfolding desolate and dreary as a misty rain pattered down, at times, even obscuring the shoulder of the road. Admittedly, Benny's eyesight was not what it once had been; so when he saw the forlorn person with a thumb out, he didn't hesitate to stop. He would soon be brought to the realization that an old man with a pocketfull of money should be more careful of the company he chooses…but by that time, of course, it was too late.

~~~~~~

It was still midmorning when a glum Charlie Yazzie looked across those same rain-soaked flats to a clearing sky. The troubled Legal Services investigator drew a deep breath and let the clean fragrance of sage wash through him. "Sage is good medicine for a *Diné*," his grandfather would say after a rain, "especially for ills of the spirit."

Maybe it was. Charlie didn't consider himself a traditionalist, but the genes were there. He forced himself to take another look at the man, now lying sprawled on his stomach, in the mud. How like his grandfather the old fellow seemed. That someone could kill so harmless a person, then leave his body dragged into a tangle of greasewood, was beyond him?"

The cause of death was obvious, even from a distance. Clearly, the old man suffered several blows to the back of the head. Charlie guessed it was with the large adjustable wrench lying next to the body. The blood and strands of hair clinging to the tool were unmistakable. Apparently, Benny had been trying to get away when brought to ground. That there was still blood on the wrench, despite overnight showers, made it clear the old fellow had, most likely, been killed sometime around daylight after the rain tapered off. Charlie Yazzie had seen a number of dead people in his years at Legal Services. Death no longer bothered him as it once had, at least not to the extent it might a more traditionally minded Navajo. He considered himself beyond that now.

There were those who felt the investigator had grown apart from his people in some regards. He had been away a long time at university—longer than most who chose that path. Some wondered if that might be the why of it. Early on, even his Aunt Annie Eagletree thought so. "There is more to life than studies that go on and on," she cautioned, afraid at the

3

time he might become one of those *professional students* she'd heard about. Later, she would become inordinately proud of her educated nephew; after all, she would say, "A tribal investigator *with* a law degree is something you don't see everyday."

Charlie's peers at Legal Services would have agreed; they considered him a shrewd and often relentless advocate for the Navajo people. This tenacity of spirit brought its own rewards—no one could dispute that—the young lawyer's rapid rise through the ranks was termed nothing less than meteoric, even by the occasional envious associate.

The investigator watched now as Navajo Tribal Policeman Billy Red Clay bulled his way through the underbrush and up onto the road. The young officer kept one eye on the ground, speaking softly into his hand-held, as he directed fellow officer Hastiin Sosi in his search of an adjacent area. Billy's grim expression mirrored his disappointment. Charlie knew the young policeman's impatience was directed inward: *the impatience of youth,* Charlie thought, yet admitted it might also be the reason Billy Red Clay had made his mark at Tribal...and on his own terms, too. He was the newly appointed liaison between Tribal Police and the FBI: a decidedly more attractive position since the previous senior agent, the arrogant Eldon Mayfield, was summarily posted elsewhere. Eldon himself admitted to being unsuited to the reservation: unable to connect with its people on any workable level. The former senior agent was convinced his considerable abilities would be more appreciated elsewhere. The man had known, from the start, that a posting to any reservation meant either a new beginning—or the beginning of the end.

The new man in charge of the Farmington division, Crime Scene Specialist Fred Smith, out of the Albuquerque office, was thought the perfect replacement. Most found Agent Smith more agreeable than his predecessor; this included the Navajo people themselves. Both Charlie Yazzie and Billy Red Clay agreed with the general consensus. Fred was a local boy, raised in San Juan County, Bloomfield in fact, and this made all the difference to their way of thinking.

Charlie still thought the name, Fred Smith, to be perfect for an FBI agent. A generic name, coupled with a forgettable face, made the man almost invisible, in his opinion. Not a bad thing, one would think, for a federal agent. Even so, few at the Bureau realized the man's potential. Fred languished for some years and was nearly thirty-five, before getting this first big break—if being posted to a reservation, even as senior agent, could be deemed a break. Perhaps it was the comparison with his predecessor that caused his new associates to think him a cut above. Local law enforcement found Fred to be intelligent and sharply intuitive, friendly without being patronizing, and apparently endowed with a passion for his calling. In short, Fred Smith was thought to be a most valuable addition to Four Corner's law enforcement. Charlie Yazzie was in that camp.

"Find anything Billy?"

The policeman brushed at his uniform, caught his breath, and finally grunted, "No, Charlie, I didn't." He knew what his friend was thinking.

At the outset, Charlie mentioned bringing in Harley Ponyboy, who he thought might be helpful. Harley was one of the few real trackers left—widely known for his ability to turn up sign where others couldn't. A person could be trained for the work, of course, but only a natural had that indefinable and elusive sixth sense. Harley was a natural.

Billy Red Clay looked up, plucked a last sprig of sage from his shirtfront, and then frowned, as though reading the investigator's mind. "I'd have called Harley Ponyboy, you know, but he doesn't have a phone, meaning someone would have to go fetch him. That would take a while." He went on, "The FBI are most likely on their way already." He said this knowing their people should have been there already. As good as the new interagency relationship appeared on the surface, the Bureau still was adamant that Tribal not disturb a homicide scene, at least not before their forensic people had a chance to work their magic.

The Feds held jurisdiction in all homicides on the reservation and, in the end, it would be the Bureau who took charge of this one. They didn't mind Tribal police securing the crime scene—were even okay with them checking out the area or interviewing witnesses—who better, after all, to sort out sign or interrogate their own people. It was all fine: as long as they didn't muck up the crime scene itself. The Bureau would make its own assessment in due course. It was typical government thinking, as far as Billy Red Clay was concerned. He had seen it in the army as well: if you were an Indian you were assumed automatically qualified as a forward scout or tracker, but any final determination in a situation was to be left to a white officer. Billy's experience as a platoon sergeant indicated this was poor thinking on the military's part.

Navajo Tribal Police had taken the call early that morning and from their own patrolman, Hastiin Sosi, making it Billy Red Clay's place to notify the FBI. He was, after all, the liaison between the two agencies.

Charlie only suggested they hold off a little, until Harley could be sent for, but Billy, in a rare instance of opposition to the tribal investigator, ultimately decided no.

"We owe it to Fred Smith." Billy was a firm believer in protocol: something else he had learned in the army. "Fred expects to be notified as quickly as possible."

The Legal Services investigator, knowing it was not his put-in, reluctantly agreed, and did not bring it up again. Charlie Yazzie himself had a long-running association with the FBI and it had not always been a happy one. He did now, however, look forward to a more transparent relationship with Agent Fred Smith. This, despite some lingering doubt as to how that might play out. He chose to remain optimistic but, at this point, still couldn't help being just a little dubious.

Charlie was well aware it was by chance alone he was allowed to ride along on the call. Tribal Police Captain Frank Beyale sat in on his reciprocal training session that morning—Spousal Abuse—a reservation problem Charlie was well acquainted with from his caseload at Legal Services. When the homicide call came in, his early morning talk was just winding up.

7

It was the captain who suggested Charlie might want to accompany Officer Red Clay.

Captain Beyale was aware the two were friends and thought the younger officer might profit from the more experienced investigator's input. This suited the Tribal policeman just fine; Charlie Yazzie had been a confidant of the young officer's mentor: Lt. Samuel Shorthair. After the Lieutenant's untimely death, the Legal Services investigator became instrumental in advancing the young *Diné's* career—at first only out of respect for Sam Shorthair. Later, however, Charlie came to realize the extent of the young officer's dedication to his job and chose to continue Sam Shorthair's interest in the young *Diné.* That Billy Red Clay was a nephew of his friend, Thomas Begay, might also have weighed in his favor.

Thomas himself was less than pleased at his nephew's choice of profession. He did, however, admit the boy seemed good at it and eventually deferred to the general opinion among his immediate clan. They thought it might be a good thing for a family member to be in such a position: there were several among them who might occasionally have need of a wink and a pass from the law. Unfortunately, that had not been the case so far with Billy Red Clay.

The report said a passing tourist stopped to let his dog out for a run that morning, and was alerted to the morbid find by the excited animal. Patrolman Hastiin Sosi, just finishing up his shift, happened by only minutes later, and was flagged down by the distraught motorist. The man said he was on his way to a Durango, Colorado art fair when the grisly encounter came about. Officer Sosi took down his information, along with where he might be reached, should that prove necessary. After assuring himself the victim was indeed dead—quite clearly the case even from a distance—Hastiin Sosi remained careful not to approach the body closer than absolutely necessary, partially due to the Navajo's inherent fear of the dead, but even more because FBI protocol demanded it. Officer Hastiin radioed Tribal for assistance.

2

The Bible Seller

The knock on metal was loud, leaving a tinny rever-beration in its wake. Harley Ponyboy turned down the radio beside him and looked up from his base-board painting. That door was on his list—loose on its hinges and prone to make strange noises when the wind was right. The little man again cocked an ear, paused his work and glanced that way, convinced now someone was indeed knocking.

The trailer's isolated location made visitors rare. The nearest neighbor was the better part of a mile away and rarely seen. *What the hell... Jake must be loose again...maybe even out on the highway?* The mule's life had already been saved, and on several occasions, by concerned passersby. Harley sighed, dropped the brush into a can of thinner and pulled himself upright by the edge of the kitchen cabinet. His back hurt, and he shrugged his shoulders a time or two for whatever relief that might bring. One foot had fallen asleep and he stomped the worn linoleum to get the circulation going. *That mule is going to make me crazy.* The animal could open most any gate should the mood strike him, or if he thought his dinner was late. Harley felt sure it would someday be the death of the lop-eared creature. Some higher intervention had thus far kept the mule off the roll of dead equines commonly found strewn along reservation highways—open range mostly—and the death count was high.

Still wiping his hands on the tail of his shirt, Harley limped to the door, tugged fiercely at the knob, then gritted his teeth at the irritating screech of metal on metal. He was left standing in the glare of the morning sun—already warm enough to make the metal door uncomfortable to the touch. Unable to focus after the cave-like interior, Harley shaded his eyes with one hand, leaving an arc of white paint just above his left brow, making him appear more surprised than he actually was. When he and his wife discussed setting the trailer, he had insisted the door should face east, right into the morning sun. She hadn't liked the idea.

"It's gonna' make this trailer a lot hotter," she said, but knew her husband's more traditional upbringing wouldn't allow it to be otherwise and was eventually forced to let it go at that.

Anita had been gone nearly two years now, and Harley tried not to think of her lest some evil come of it. She hadn't been a particularly kindhearted woman even when alive.

Harley narrowed a cautious eye at the person on the steps—a girl, he thought—now turned toward the highway and possibly thinking no one was home. He blinked a time or two, surprised at so unlikely a visit, and unable to fathom what might have brought her there. He had seen local Girl Scouts selling cookies in Shiprock only the day before, but couldn't imagine one venturing so far from town just to sell a box of Thin Mints. If she was a scout, she was out of uniform. The short red dress and elevated heels were eye catching, but somehow out of place there on the rickety front porch of an old trailer house in the wilds of the *Dinétah.*

She turned and contemplated Harley with a boldness that unsettled him. Her small stature was deceiving; it was clear now she wasn't a girl at all—hadn't been one for some years, he guessed. Harley professed no particular skill in guessing the ages of women. He, in fact, knew very little about women despite his years of marriage. About the time he thought he had one figured out, he would be proven wrong, not just occasionally, but almost every time.

"I'm selling Bibles," the woman said, patting her shoulder bag as she looked him over.

He felt the heat rise to his face and remained uncertain how to address this obvious intent to sell him a Bible. He didn't want a Bible nor did he have money for one. Women made Harley nervous; and a female Bible salesman fell totally outside his comfort range. His mind stalled momentarily unable to come up with an excuse that didn't sound foolish. Despite the red hair, the woman appeared to be at least half-Indian. She had almost no accent, leading Harley to conclude she might be any sort of Indian. He was about to ask if she was *Diné,* but she interrupted before the words could leave his mouth.

"Are you the man of the house?" She was aware men were occasionally rendered speechless in her presence and thought it might be due to her bold manner. She'd often found this an advantage. "Maybe I should speak to your wife?"

Harley glanced sideways at her, frowned, and momentarily lost the power of speech. They stared at one another. "I don't have a wife no more," he said finally. Then plucking up his courage, "And I do not need a Bible, thank you," and then in a confidential aside, "I am not really a religious person."

The woman raised an eyebrow—touching the tip of her tongue to her teeth while thinking this over. She shrugged finally, admitting, "I'm not very religious myself." She almost smiled as she went on, "A person doesn't have to be religious to sell Bibles, or to buy one...thank God." She held up a forefinger and took a sterner tack. "The thing is..." and here she paused to recall exactly what the thing should be. "Everyone should have a Bible," she said, recapturing her train of thought, "...in case the need arises to *become* religious." She looked directly at him, "Many a damned heathen changes their mind in a bad situation and feels the want of a Bible." Her tone softened and a light seemed to play across her features. "I was religious once, when I was young. I thought I wanted to be a Mormon...I tried but it never quite took." She lowered a conspiratorial eyelid. "My father was white and a Mormon convert. Maybe still is...but I somehow doubt it. I don't think *he* was cut out for it either. He damned sure wasn't cut out to be a father." She blew a strand of tousled red hair from one eye and moved closer, right up in Harley's face. "The point is—a person never knows when something terrible might befall him and cause him to find comfort in the

Word." She nodded knowingly. "I'll bet you could have used a Bible when you lost your wife."

Harley, though somewhat taken aback at this plain talk, gathered himself. "No, I was drunk at the time...stayed drunk for a long while after... I never really felt the need of a Bible." He poked his head beyond the safety of the door to look around, then changed the subject. "No car? How did you get here?"

"I had an old car...but the bastard broke down over by Tonalea...ran out of oil I guess...blew a rod right through the pan." She smiled, "I got fifty bucks for it." She seemed to consider this. "I guess you have to check the oil a little more often than I thought." The woman then frowned—mentally lamenting the fact the buyer would probably have given more if she'd had the title. *It was unfair,* she thought, *the car cost eight hundred dollars only the month before.* She'd had to sell a lot of Bibles just to make the down payment

Harley, too, frowned, still not sure how the woman got there. After thinking a moment, Harley, ever the master of the obvious, remarked, "Tonalea is a long way."

"Tell me about it," the woman grimaced. "I caught a ride to Kayenta. After that I was damned lucky to find another. I had to hang out at the Chevron station for quite a while before an old woman stopped for gas. She took me a little farther...almost to Dinnehotso. One of her daughters had been thinking of going to her cousin's place at Mexican Water for a party. The daughter said, if I could chip in a couple of bucks for gas, she thought we could make it." The woman stopped and twirled a strand of red hair around a forefinger, watching carefully to see how this man was taking her story. Satisfied, she went on, "When we got there, her cousin offered to let me spend the night with them, but I didn't like the looks of those people, so I hit the road again; it was almost daylight before I caught another ride." She smiled as she looked toward the distant highway. "Not much traffic out there today, is there?" Then, "The man who brought me this far said he was your neighbor...something Nakii... said you might be going into town today. He told me he would take me on in himself but he didn't have enough gas in his truck to make it as far as that."

Harley smiled, "That would be Alfred Nakii; he doesn't have much money." Harley assured her of this in a way he hoped would excuse his friend. "He only got out of jail about a month ago." Harley shook his head in mild disbelief. "Six months just for stealing a little burro and two goats! That's crazy. The judge said he wouldn't have gone so hard on him if he hadn't already eaten one of them."

"I can understand that. A lot of people like goat."

"No. It was the burro, or at least a good bit of it, before they finally came for him. It was a small burro, not really good for anything, according to Alfred. He told me it was a mean little so-and-so, too, said he couldn't do a thing with it. It tried to kick him every chance and honked and beeped so loud it was getting on his nerves. He told me he had only taken it along in the first place because it refused to leave the goats—wouldn't stop braying when he tried to lead them off. One of the goats was milking pretty well, and he thought the other one might be pregnant.

Those two were worth keeping, he said. He told the judge he was just trying to get a little herd started and planned to replace those animals when he'd raised a few. He also mentioned their owner had more animals than he could feed; he said the man's pasture was worn out. The way he looked at it, he was doing him a favor. He'd winked at the judge as he said all this, thinking it might help."

Harley, relaxing now against the door jam, took his time. "Alfred, never being arrested before, and not really knowing how things worked, decided the judge might appreciate knowing some of these things he was telling him. I guess later he figured out that wasn't the case." Harley stopped to consider his friend. "Alfred's not a bad guy, he's not. He probably just got off on the wrong foot with that burro."

Harley scratched his head. "When I was a kid people around here used to eat wild burro all the time. There were plenty of them in those days and the deer were nearly all shot out. Burro's good eating when you know how to fix it. I like it better than deer myself."

Harley was on a roll and couldn't quit talking. There was something about this woman... "The sad thing was...Alfred's mother died while he was still in jail. He was a good son and had always lived right there at home with his mom. He was a big help to the old lady as she got older, everyone could see that." The little man gave a sad shake of his head. "Not long ago Alfred told me he sometimes feels responsible for her death—said he'd maybe been the cause of it—being in jail and all. He thought maybe him being gone made her so sad she just gave up and died."

Harley made that little tsk, tsk, tsk, sound people
sometimes do when they think something's a shame.
"Alfred lives over there all by himself now...he had a
dog... but it died too." He brightened momentarily.
"He's been looking for a wife but hasn't had much
luck so far. He owns that trailer up there outright you
know...did he mention that? He's an okay
guy...really." Harley Ponyboy was one of those people who are prone to see the best in everyone; he just
couldn't help it.

"Well, I guess all that's good to know." The
woman murmured, looking furtively about, her gaze
finally settling on Harley's truck. "Maybe it's not as
quiet out here as I thought." She eyed the meandering
dirt track back to the highway with a tired sigh.

"Oh, no...it's usually pretty quiet out this way."
Harley insisted. "We don't get much traffic even during the day...none at night." He raised an eyebrow
causing the white paint to, again, offer the impression
of a person in a state of surprise. "Are you from
around here?" He knew she wasn't. He would have
remembered her if she was. He'd never seen anyone
quite like her. She was striking. There was a bit of an
edge to her perhaps, but in that interesting way some
men find attractive.

While mulling these things over it finally occurred to Harley the woman must be tired and
probably thirsty. He had forgotten his manners and
quickly thought to make amends. "Would you like to
come in out of the sun and rest a minute...have a
drink of water, maybe?" He again wiped his hands on
his shirttail, explaining, "I'm painting the baseboards
right now but I'll be going into Shiprock later on to-

day." Harley gestured nervously toward the unfinished trim. "It's oil-base...so I need ta keep after it." He hesitated, half-turning in the doorway to contemplate the work in progress then explained, "I'm goin' ta need more paint later on." Then looked away as he mumbled, "I could maybe give you a lift that far if you wanted?"

"That your truck over there?" The woman's glance was calculating but turned doubtful as she continued her study of the pickup.

This caused Harley to look at the vehicle in a new light himself, as though seeing it for the first time. "Well, I've only had it a year or so. I'm trying ta fix it up as I get the money. It runs okay but the passenger door pops open sometimes when it hits a bump...a person has ta be careful about that...and it needs tires, too. I have a little list Thomas Begay made for me of all the things it needs. He's a mechanic." Harley turned back into the trailer and motioned for her to follow.

The woman, shaking her head behind his back, followed him into the house. Despite the work in progress she was surprised at how orderly everything seemed; *a woman must have spent some time training this man.* She did not, for the most part, consider herself a good housekeeper, but admired the trait in others.

Harley hesitated. "So...what is your name, if you don't mind me asking?" He was pretty good at remembering names and kept them filed away for years sometimes—a few of them forever. That was one of the things that made it hard to forget Anita.

"No...I...don't mind at all," She said, adjusting her shoulder bag. "It's Eileen...Eileen...Smith."

Harley accepted this in the spirit it was offered. "You're part Indian. Right?" He hoped this wasn't out of line. Some people didn't want to be seen as part Indian...but that was mostly just the ones who actually were.

"Yep, *Dinè*, just like you Mr...?"

"Ah, sorry about that. I'm Harley...Harley Ponyboy. Do you speak any Navajo?"

"Not much. My father didn't allow it. But after he left home I picked up a little from my mother and her sister. They didn't think I had much of a knack for it, probably figured it was the white blood. My mother didn't know that much of it herself, at least from what I saw when *her* father came to see us; it was almost like she could hardly understand him sometimes...or he, her. My Aunt Mary is older and a little better at it." Eileen was peeking into the trailer's front bedroom. "A two bedroom, huh? That's nice..." She knew a lot about old trailer houses—had, in fact, lived in several herself and had always been partial to the front bedroom models.

"There's another bedroom in the back. My wife always kept it made up in case any of her relatives came to visit, but she was on the outs with her family most of the time, so none of them ever came." Harley cleared his throat and said, "I used to drink a little and when I did, she made me sleep back there so as not to disturb her too much." Harley then went on to reassure the woman. "I don't drink hardly at all, anymore." A sad little look passed over him. "I should have quit when she was still alive…maybe she'd still be here if I had."

Eileen smiled into the mirror over the couch and touched her hair. "Well, I've heard that story more than a few times, Harley. Hindsight's great, isn't it?" She turned and tilted her head, "What was her name?"

"I don't like to say her name…I don't want ta take the chance."

"Ummm," *…an old-school Navajo, funny how so many still thought like this. Even those who moved away to white towns and no longer spoke the language; they still held on to the old beliefs.* Her mother once told her it was like *Diné* Alzheimer's—they forget everything but the superstitions.

Harley changed the subject, "There's plenty of water in the tank if you might like ta wash up or anything. It should be warm about now. You can take a shower if you like…that door locks." Harley was more than a little proud of the water system. He and his friend Thomas Begay had put it in years back—even before he had electricity—and it worked fine as long he remembered to fill the tank every week or so. It was an old farm tank on a tall stand at the back of the trailer. They had picked it up for cheap at the salvage yard in Farmington, painted it black, and then angled it to catch the sun for the better part of the day. After they got the fuel smell out (and that hadn't been easy) Thomas Begay began calling it a Navajo water heater. Both men thought it quite an improvement, what with being off the grid and all. Later when Harley *did* get electricity he had to drop in a floating horse tank heater in order to keep using it through the winter. For a while there he and Thomas thought of going into business, selling and installing such tanks, but they were drinking at the time, so nothing ever came of it.

Eileen looked down at her clothes and shook her head to the offer. "Oh...well, about that...one of my rides drove off with my suitcase," she lied, "so I really don't have anything else to wear right now."

Harley nodded, as though this was a common enough thing to have happen, then after thinking said, "There's some of Ani...some of my wife's clothes still in the back closet; if any of them fit, you are welcome to them. I have been meaning to take them ta the Goodwill store anyway. She was some bigger than you but you can take a look and see what you think."

The woman eyed the little man, and thought this over, finally concluding he was what he appeared to be: an honest human being trying to help. She hadn't known many but thought this might be one.

~~~~~~~

Harley finished out the last of his paint, and washed up before he started fixing a light lunch of fried Spam and eggs. There were some tortillas too. He figured they'd be okay once they were warmed up. He augmented the morning's coffee grounds with the last of the Folgers then added water and set the pot on a back burner. He hadn't expected a guest for lunch but couldn't have done much better even if he had. He and Thomas Begay had both been idle the last week and money was short. It might be yet another week before Professor Custer returned to put them back to work.

He was just about to put the eggs in the skillet when he heard the shower running. He smiled to himself, set the Spam on the back of the stove, and decided to hold off on the eggs. He moved the radio from the floor to the kitchen cabinet, plugged it in beside the refrigerator and clicked it on.

When he turned it to KTNN—Voice of The Navajo Nation—he heard the intro signaling the noon news segment: fifteen minutes of news in Navajo. The announcer rattled through a few national headlines then launched into a local, "Bulletin just in…" concerning the discovery of a body—that of an elderly man—just west of the New Mexico state line—on Highway 64. Identification of the victim had not been released pending notification of next of kin. Authorities said foul play couldn't be ruled out. The announcer's voice turned upbeat as he assured listeners further information would follow on the regional news at five.

Harley filed this information away in the back of his mind and determined not to miss the evening report. He knew people up in that area, clan members mostly, and hoped this old man didn't turn out to be one of them. He was still mulling the report over when he heard the bathroom door open and Eileen, wearing his late wife's too-large house slippers, shuffled down the hall from the back bedroom.

Harley turned to the stove and set the eggs to frying then opened the still warm oven to remove a stack of corn tortillas wrapped in a tea towel. The coffee pot was perking away.

"That smells good."

"Well, it's not much. I haven't been ta the store in a while."

Eileen, when he glanced back at her, had piled her long hair on top of her head and wrapped it in a towel. She looked taller this way even with just the slippers. She hung her book bag on the back of a chair then turned a pirouette while holding out her arms. She had discovered a sweatshirt and running pants in the closet, all too big, but they looked all right on her somehow.

"It's about ready…pull up a chair." Harley wanted to say she looked nice, but wasn't sure he could put the words together in such a way it didn't sound like he was hitting on her. The table was set and he brought the coffee pot over to fill their cups.

Eileen knit her brows in a show of concern. "I maybe used more water than I should have. It just felt so good I couldn't bring myself to turn it off." She put a hand on his and smiled. "I appreciate this Harley…I know how hard water is to come by out here." She smiled again—what Harley took to be a genuine reflection of her thanks.

"Don't you worry about that, Eileen. I'll get another load of water this afternoon in Shiprock. It's free from the community pump; we just have ta go get it."

They ate in silence for a few minutes: Eileen complimenting his cooking, which embarrassed him a little, but made him feel good at the same time. "So, Eileen, were you in Phoenix long?"

She lifted an eyebrow. "How did you know I was in Phoenix?"

"Uh...it's on the back of your bag," he said pointing. "Phoenix Bible Outreach Center." Harley didn't mention the small, almost indiscernible print near the bottom: Halfway House for A Better Future.

"I was in Phoenix for a while...couple of years I guess."

Harley didn't change expression, just went on eating and nodding his head as he thought this over, finally looking up to say, "Your business is your business, Eileen. You don't need to tell me any of it if it bothers you."

Eileen put down her fork and smoothed her hair. "There's very little that bothers me anymore Harley Ponyboy, I've grown used to who I am and where I've been."

Harley was now even more intrigued by this woman who didn't pretend to be other than what she was—regardless of what that might turn out to be. "Right after we eat we can load up the water barrels and head into town."

"You know, Harley, I'd rather just stay here if you don't mind. It will give me a chance to wash my clothes and get myself in order...maybe even take a little nap." She reached into her bag and took out some bills and handed them to him. "Pick up some food in town...I like to pay my way," she said, "and I won't take no for an answer." Her words had an air of finality that gave the little man pause. "Oh," she continued, "if you don't mind, could you pick me up a bottle of black hair dye? I'm tired of this red mop."

Harley accepted the money without a word and put it in his pocket without counting. He had secretly admired her long red hair but guessed all along it wasn't natural…or was it? In any case he didn't feel it was his place to offer an opinion on something she had obviously already decided.

"I'll clean this up while you're gone," she said, with a wave of her hand at the kitchen.

"I shouldn't be gone too long, Eileen, I'll try to pick out something good for supper. Is there anything special you had in mind?" He thought this the polite thing seeing how she was paying. He found it pleasant having so congenial a conversation, and with a woman who was obviously better educated than he. Anita had not been inclined to small talk; her reluctance sometimes causing her to come off as querulous or hard to please.

"You do that, Harley. I guess I wouldn't mind having some pork chops if you happen to run across any nice ones."

Harley smiled agreeably and tried not to sound obsequious. "I like pork chops, too, Eileen. I'll see what I can find, and if not, I'll get what does look good." Harley, for the first time in weeks, was showing some consideration for another person—even if it *was* only what he should make for dinner. He had already guessed he would probably be the one doing the cooking.

3

The Quandary

Back at Legal Services, Charlie Yazzie still couldn't get his mind off the murder of the old man. There was something about it that stuck in his craw—leaving him determined to keep abreast of any new developments in the case. This, though he still hadn't been invited to take an active part.

About noon, he called home to see how his friend, Thomas Begay, was coming along with their new tractor project. Charlie and his friends had been looking to go in on a small tractor for some time now, and when Harley Ponyboy found a machine the right size in an upcoming farm auction, the three decided it might just be the one. They had missed a similar tractor the week before in Aztec and didn't intend to let this one slip by. Thomas thought this machine might prove even more of a bargain considering it was being offered at auction in Bloomfield.

The auctioneer's stickman told the crowd the previous owner assured them the tractor ran fine last season. But, when it came time for the machine to sell, a vigorous session of cranking left the tractor stubbornly refusing to start. Employees were forced to call on the owner to pull it into the ring with his Jeep. The man continued cursing the tractor as he unhooked it. Charlie and Harley Ponyboy stood with their arms folded, now convinced the previous owner had expected the tractor to start. They took this as a good sign. Thomas, having surveyed the machine prior to the start of the auction, nodded wisely but kept his own council.

It was agreed the three would go in as partners—more of a theoretical partnership as Charlie was the only one with any money. Thomas, on the other hand, was the one with expertise in mechanics and in charge of getting the unit operating. He was quick to assure the others there was nothing seriously wrong with it. He pointed to the fact that there were no leaks in the hydraulics; he'd checked the radiator for oil in the water; the crankcase for water in the oil and, finding none of these to be suspicious indicators, encouraged Charlie to start the bid. He went so far as to guess the tractor would now go even cheaper— what with it not starting.

Most of the other bidders were, in fact, cautious of a tractor that wouldn't run, and the competition quickly faded, leaving Charlie Yazzie the winning bidder and at a very favorable price.

Thomas, stroking his chin, assured his partners it was a steal and he would have the little diesel running in no time.

Harley Ponyboy's input was slight during the process, as he had neither expertise nor money to offer, but he took solace in the fact that he did at least know how to drive a tractor, something Charlie Yazzie was, as yet, unskilled at.

Later in the day, Charlie's wife, Sue, went to the window and called Thomas Begay to the phone, telling him her husband wanted to speak to him.

Only a few minutes into the conversation Thomas was forced to admit, "No, I don't have it running yet..." thus betraying his original assertion of an easy fix.

Charlie was not happy with this development. "You said that tractor would be no problem to get running." All the while, knowing Sue was apt to be listening to the conversation. She had been against the idea of a tractor, for so small an acreage as theirs, from the very start. They had a new baby girl, she had reminded him, and bills to pay. She was of the opinion she should have been consulted before Thomas came dragging the thing into the yard on a flatbed trailer.

Sue edged over closer to Thomas and the phone. "This sounds like another one of those grown-boy toys *someone* can play farmer with." She offered this in a voice calculated for Charlie to hear. Then in an even louder tone, added, "We haven't even done our taxes yet..." indicating the hoped-for refund was little more than imaginary at this point.

Thomas held the phone in such a way his friend could better hear what they were up against.

Charlie sat silent on the other end of the line—weighing the fact that he had put up all the money for the machine—at least until the other two could afford to pitch in on it. He then sighed and decided to let the issue lie until evening by which time he hoped to mount a proper defense. Before he hung up, he did, however, ask Thomas Begay to drop by his office on his way home.

Thomas sheepishly replaced the receiver and, still not looking at Sue, wondered out loud if she had a phone book: there were some parts he might need.

Sue thought this an additional cautionary indicator and glared out the window with folded arms before finally saying, "Humph!" and passing him the directory.

In the meantime, little Joseph Wiley came out of a bedroom where he had been playing quietly with his baby sister, Sasha. The five-year-old boy silently considered his mother from a distance, and then wisely decided against asking for cookies.

~~~~~~~

Thomas arrived at Charlie's office just past quitting time. He'd planned it that way in case the conversation grew heated...something he thought likely. The two had been friends since their days at the BIA boarding facility in Aztec and were prone to tell one another exactly what was on their minds. He slipped into the outer office as the last of the office personnel were leaving. When he knocked politely at the glass window of Charlie's office—a rare form of etiquette for Thomas, and one he seldom employed—he could see Charlie on the phone; chair swiveled toward the window. The investigator apparently hadn't heard him and he knocked again, more forcefully this time. Charlie turned his head, looked over his shoulder, and ushered him in with a flip of a hand.

Thomas stood quietly for a moment, listening to the conversation. Charlie was doing most of the talking and obviously didn't care who overheard. From what Thomas could gather some old man's truck had been found in Farmington, parked on a side street, behind a bar frequented by Indians. When he heard the name of the place mentioned he had to chuckle—he was familiar with the establishment—was, in fact, an old customer before he quit drinking. It was the sort of dive he and Harley Ponyboy favored back in those times and he could recall several unpleasant experiences there—at least one of which led to jail time. The specifics of that incident were now unclear, as were so many things from his drinking days. It made him uncomfortable now, to think back on those times, knowing he had often been the instigator and responsible for both he and his friend Harley spending time as guests of San Juan County. The charges were never very serious, in his estimation, but enough to make them both fairly well known to local law enforcement.

Charlie Yazzie whipped his chair around, with a loud squeak, interrupting Thomas's trip down memory lane. Thomas watched as the investigator clunked the phone down in its cradle; he frowned as he watched him sift through a stack of papers.

Neither man spoke: each thinking he had a pretty good idea what the other would say, and usually that would have been the case, but not this time.

Charlie raised an eyebrow. "Don't you have some clan up around Teec Nos Pos?

This threw the tall *Diné* for just a moment. He had been concentrating on excuses for why the tractor wasn't fixed and now had to rearrange his thinking. He paused to consider, before saying, "Naw, that would be Harley. I think there's a little knot of Reed People up there, somewhere, he's related to. Those people move around a lot."

Charlie chewed on this for a moment. "Tribal Police have a homicide on their hands…well, I guess the FBI have it by now. An old man named Benny Klee…from around Teec Nos Pos. His body was found just past the New Mexico state line." The investigator shifted in his chair and pulled a paper closer to him. "I was up there this morning with your nephew, Billy Red Clay. Apparently, someone killed this…Benny Klee… and stole his pickup. The county cops just found the truck in Farmington with the keys still in the ignition. Whoever took it knew not to keep it very long. The interior had been wiped down, too, and the license plate was so muddy you couldn't read the numbers."

"Sounds like it wasn't the guy's first time out of the chute."

"That's what I'm thinking. I figured maybe you and I could slip into town and talk to a few people who hang out at that bar."

Thomas smiled broadly. "FBI be damned, and off the record, you mean?" He studied his friend's neatly pressed shirt and shiny boots. "No one's going to talk to you down there, college boy. Those people can spot a cop a mile away." Thomas then looked down at his own greasy Levi's jeans and diesel stained shirt. "Now me… I might have a chance. It's been a while since I was a part of that bunch, though. I might have to get my credit re-established." He grinned at the look on his friend's face. "Just kidding, Charlie. I'm good with the way I'm living now…drinking's not part of who I am anymore." He stopped and narrowed one eye at the ceiling. "I wish I could say the same for Harley. I haven't seen him in a couple of days now and I'm a little worried. Last I saw of him was at the Co-op, buying more stuff to fix up that old trailer of his. He said his money was about gone but he might as well use what he had left fixing up the place. Just something for him to do until we go back to work for George, I suppose."

"What's Professor Custer up to? I thought he had work lined up for you two, through the summer at least."

"We thought so, too." Thomas smiled. "The work is there, all right; the professor just took a few days off. He's up in Cortez trying to talk Aida Winters into marrying him." He chuckled, "Apparently it's turned into more of a chore than he thought."

Charlie sat back in his chair, uneasy at the thought of his old friend setting himself up for so likely a disappointment. "George mentioned he had been thinking about making a final run at that situation, but I didn't think he would actually do it." He shook his head and turned back toward the window. "He and Aida didn't part on the best of terms last year, at least that's what I hear from Sue…who heard it from *your* wife by the way." Charlie didn't quite know what to make of his old professor: the man seemed to be at loose ends despite his new business.

"I suspect George has been lonely." The investigator stood and stretched, then turned again to the office window where he watched what was left of the afterhours traffic trickle past. He canted his head and smiled. "Harley came by the house two or three days ago...said he was there to drop off that ladder I loaned him. He stayed to wrangle dinner; I think *he's* lonely, too. That boy needs to find a woman."

Thomas chuckled, "Well, you know Harley's never been lucky when it comes to women; he don't have a clue how to go about it."

Charlie couldn't argue with that. "I thought for a while things might be different, now that Anita's been gone as long as she has. But I'm beginning to lose hope he'll ever find anyone."

"I know...Lucy tried to line him up with one of our neighbor women from the chapter house. Nice young woman with a good job at Child Services. She just bought a new pickup truck, too." Thomas sniffed. "Harley said she wasn't his type." Then snorted, "When Lucy got a little huffy with him and asked what he thought *his* type was, he would only say, 'I'll know her when I see her.' Which is about what I would expect him to say." The tall *Diné* shook his head. "Lucy told him he's going to wind up an old maid, if he's not careful." Both men laughed at this, but privately, each wondered if Lucy might be right.

~~~~~~

The red, faded-to-pink, neon sign read, San Juan Social Club. A painted banner across the window was lettered, Bar and Lounge, and beneath that, a fly specked placard in one corner declared—Indians Welcome. Thomas parked his diesel truck well up the street from, what he referred to as, The Establishment. When he turned to Charlie, it was with a serious tone. "I really think you ought to stay in the truck. No offense, *hastiin*, but I expect I can learn more in there without you."

Charlie glanced again at the placard, and with a tentative smile, asked, "Are you saying I can't *pass?*"

"Pretty much…" Thomas wasn't smiling when he said it either. "Some of those old boys in there are the real deal when it comes to rough and tough, and we didn't come down here to scare the hell out of ourselves."

Charlie thought it unlikely there was anyone inside the bar that could scare the hell out of Thomas Begay, but could only nod and agree, "Whatever you say *hastiin,* we're in your bailiwick now."

When Thomas got down from the truck, he paused, one hand still on the handle. "Of course, if you see a big dust cloud come boiling out the door you can come a running. I doubt you'll need a gun, but that badge might come in handy."

A low bank of clouds was moving in from the northwest making for a somber and humid end to a day that started out bright and sunny. Even so, Thomas had to give his eyes a moment to adjust to the dimly lit room as he threaded his way through a scatter of round tables dwarfed by a massive bar: a leftover relic of Farmington's early boom days, when the place was considered *exclusive*, meaning Indians were not welcome. Back in those days, the oil field elite stood watch over the sanctity of Farmington's exclusive watering holes. Clientele included oil execs, engineers, and suddenly wealthy scions of the emerging energy industry. But then was then, now was now. The drilling had slowed considerably over the intervening years leaving mostly work-over rigs and fracking units to ply their trade through the isolated vastness of the Four Corner's gas fields.

Over the bar, now, was a life-size painting of an Indian chief in full feather headdress; one hand held up to the patrons. At the bottom of the picture was the pronouncement, "We have Reservations!"

Thomas had seen the picture a number of times and in each instance a different interpretation came to mind. Every one of them made him smile.

Behind the polished mahogany bar a familiar figure leaned on both elbows watching silently as Thomas approached. A smile flickered across the woman's broad features causing her black eyes to dance. She was huge, dark, with one long braid down her back. A squash-blossom necklace fell nearly to the bar; it was clear she remembered Thomas.

"Well, Begay, I see you have finally come back to us after all. I guess those stories I heard about you quitting were wrong?" The woman grimaced as she lifted her bulk away from the bar to stand up straight—all six feet of her. She slammed a trucker-size fist on the bar. "You owe me money!"

Thomas held up both hands, stepped back and grinned. "I can't owe you money, Big'un; you never give me any credit."

"No, but that last time they hauled your ass off to jail you left owing me eight dollars—you and Harley Playboy." She glared. "Harley came by a long time

35

ago and paid his part. Didn't he give you the message I sent?"

"Not that I recall Rosie...but that's when Harley was drinking...he might have forgot." He smiled, "What was the message?"

"The message was, 'I'm going to kick your ass up between your shoulder blades the next time you show up in here.' "

Several nearby patrons turned, attracted by this rough talk. They had often seen Rosie transform such a statement into action and that most always proved entertaining.

Rosie Johnson glanced down the bar and waved a warning hand at the eavesdroppers, causing them to immediately turn their attention elsewhere. Not one was willing to become a part of the entertainment should the situation turn ugly. The big Ute woman smiled thinly at Thomas and softened her tone, "...but I expect that's why you've finally dropped by...ain't that right, Begay?"

Thomas dug in his pocket and produced a crumpled five-dollar bill and held it out to the woman. "That extra dollar's a tip Rosie." When she didn't smile he ignored it with a straight face. "I'd have settled this before now but I was probably too drunk to remember owing it. I haven't been handy to town lately any way...I been working a camp job."

Rosie plucked the bill from his hand and smoothed it on the bar. "Those past warrants starting to stack up are they, Begay?" She grinned and beckoned for him to come closer, then leaned back across the bar and in a conspiratorial tone assured him, "I always knew one day I'd look up and see you coming

to pay me—you were always good for your word—
we go back a long way, me and you." She winked
and nodded in such a manner as to make Thomas
nervous, thinking there might be something else he
didn't remember.

"Now, what can I get you?"

"Only a little information, Rosie. There was an
old man found dead, just this side of the state line this
morning. They located his truck parked across that
vacant lot behind the bar—cops already towed it now,
I guess. I just wondered if you might know anything
about that...or maybe seen someone in here today,
someone you didn't know, or a person acting funny;
you know I what mean, Rosie?"

The big woman inclined her head even closer
and then, closing one eye, she whispered, "You
wouldn't be pimping for the cops would you, Begay?"

"You know me, Rosie. I don't talk to cops."

She nodded and rubbed her chin, "That's a
fact...as far as I know...but things have a way of
changing, don't they?" She stepped back with a dis-
arming smile. "The cops already asked me about the
truck...early this morning. I told them, same as I'm
telling you, I don't know a damn thing about it.
Didn't see nothin—don't know nothin."

Thomas stood, quietly, knowing this was her last
word on the matter; he raised both hands in resigna-
tion and turned to go.

The woman's voice hardened behind him.
"Don't ever come back in here Begay. I don't know
what your game is...but I don't want you running it
in my place."

Thomas nodded. "Not a problem, Rosie..." then stopped to look back. "Are we good now; me and you?"

She frowned. "We're good...but we're through... I don't want to see you back in here."

As Thomas moved toward the door, a man at a nearby table came slowly to his feet, put money down, and then shrugged into his Levi jacket. He reached the door just before Thomas Begay, and outside, stopped for a moment right in front of him—like he'd forgotten something, or maybe changed his mind and decided to go back inside. He was taller than average, thin, and well past middle age; his hair tied in a traditional bun at the nape of his neck. Thomas, not really paying attention, didn't at first recognize him but when he half-turned and spoke, Thomas instantly knew him. The man spoke again, voice lower this time, gravelly and rough. In old Navajo, he whispered in that direct way someone might address a stranger.

"I guess you don't know me no more, huh, *Gah*?"

Thomas stared at this man who knew he was called Rabbit as a boy. "I know you all right...what's it been, thirty years?"

"Maybe," the man coughed. "I can't keep track so good anymore."

"No, Gilbert, you were never very good at keeping track." Thomas knew it was something his father chose not to remember.

The man's eyes were red-rimmed and rheumy in the dim light and he stared back at Thomas, seeming to take his measure after all these years, possibly comparing him to how he once was as a boy. He wavered, seeming less certain, as he noticed Charlie Yazzie sitting in the truck just up the street—obviously watching.

Thomas thought, for a moment, his father was about to walk off...but he only straightened, and looking past him, studied the person in the truck. He seemed determined now to stand his ground. "I overheard you talking to the barmaid in there..." The man's voice trailed off as he looked, bleary-eyed, at the door they'd just come out of, then thought of something else. "Uh...you got a couple of bucks you can spare?" He said this last part in English and couldn't keep from licking his lips as he glanced back toward the bar.

Thomas knew the look, and he knew what the man was thinking too, but only asked. "Did you hear something I ought to know?"

"Maybe. Earlier in there, before you come in, there was a man asking around if anyone had seen a *ghaw-jih* in there," the old man used the derogatory word for mixed-breed. " 'She is a small woman with red hair,' he said, and asked again if anyone knew of such a woman. 'She'd be a stranger...maybe just come into town the last day or so?' " He paused, looked again toward Charlie Yazzie and his tone grew suspicious. "Is that a friend of yours in that truck up there?"

"Never mind about him, he's no one you need to worry about." Thomas's voice took a sudden edge. "Did this man say what the woman's name was?" and when Gilbert didn't answer, asked sharply, "What else did he say?"

39

"No, he didn't mention no name. He said that probably wouldn't mean anything now. But he did say he was offering a reward for information on her whereabouts. He seemed pretty flush, too; I seen him give the barmaid money, and it looked like a good bit." He put a hand on Thomas's arm. "You know you can't trust that Ute woman in there, *Gah*? She'll throw you in the river for sure if she can." Then Gilbert put his hand out palm up and lifted his chin in a little jerk toward the bar.

Thomas pulled out his last dollar bills and passed them over in the flickering glow of the neon sign. He thought his father looked even more frail and vulnerable as he took the money. The wind was kicking up and had a bite to it. A frontal system hung north of the La Plata and it was on the move. "You better go somewhere else to spend that. Someone inside may have seen us talking."

The old man appeared momentarily doubtful—possibly unsure he could make it to the next bar—only blocks away. He finally nodded that he understood and, pulling up the collar of his jacket, turned up the street, then quickly made his way down an alley. Thomas watched him go wondering if this might be the last time he ever saw him. He thought he should feel more emotion but there was nothing left inside for Gilbert anymore. He'd heard he was back in town, but hadn't expected to see him…and certainly not like this…there was just nothing left.

Thomas had been only nine or ten the night Gilbert Nez walked out on them—saying he was going to follow the Rodeo Circuit. He assured them he'd be back when he'd made a stake. The three of them were at the Intertribal Ceremonials in Gallup. Thomas and his mother were there to watch him ride; at the time, they believed Gilbert could do anything. He won the All-Around Champion Cowboy title that night. But those all-Indian rodeos weren't Pro-Rodeo and the money hadn't lasted long in the back-alley bars of Gallup.

Charlie kicked open the truck door for his friend and slid back over to the passenger side. He had been listening to the radio as he watched and waited, and he saw Thomas's shoulders slump as he turned toward the pickup.

When the tall *Diné* folded in behind the wheel, he sat motionless, staring out the windshield as he drummed a finger on the steering wheel.

Charlie turned a curious eye. "Who was the old man?"

Thomas looked over at him and his voice grew soft when he said. "He's not nobody now...but by God, one night when I was a kid in Gallup, he was the All Around Champion Cowboy."

Charlie Yazzie knew instantly who he was talking about. He'd heard that story a number of times when they were in government boarding school. Thomas talked a lot about his father back then...back when he still thought the man might someday come home.

"He'll come rolling in sometime when we least expect it," Thomas would say. "Probably driving a new truck and his pockets full of money."

Charlie turned to the side window, quiet, waiting for his friend to get his mind right.

41

When Thomas spoke again, it was about the business at hand. That other thing, already back inside its box, was locked up good and tight. He squared his shoulders, put the truck in gear, and at the next stoplight turned to Charlie with a grin. "Hell, you could of come along with me in there, college boy. I couldn't have done any worse if you'd been right alongside. Rosie had me pegged from the get-go. She hasn't worked that bar all these years without learning a thing or two." He chuckled, "In the old days a lot of people thought she'd go under after her husband, Chuck, died. But not me, I knew from the start she was the one who kept that place going." Chuck was a big, rough-talking white man but he was a drunk, too, and a slow thinker. Rosie's not either one of those things."

Thomas saw the light change, tapped his horn at the car in front of them. "It's green!" he said under his breath. "You dumb bastard," and then let the clutch out. The big diesel jerked forward and the car in front skittered away like a rabbit. "Rosie might be getting in a little over her head on this one though. She knows something and thinks she has all her bases covered." He then went on to tell Charlie Yazzie everything that took place, both in the bar and outside with his old man.

Charlie whistled softly under his breath and looked over at his friend. "Still, none of this may have anything to do with the death of Benny Klee. Whoever killed him and left his pickup here in town may be in Albuquerque by now...or wherever he was headed when he killed Benny."

Thomas nodded, "Maybe so, but there's still something about this deal that makes me think this guy came here on purpose...I think he's still around all right. He's not going to leave until he finds this woman he's looking for."

The investigator mulled this over as he watched his friend from the corner of his eye. *Thomas isn't anyone's fool and he has a lot more street time with this sort of people than I do. He could be on to something.* Charlie rolled down his window and noticed the wind had died...leaving only enough breeze to spin a paper cup along the gutter.

R. Allen Chappell

4

The Hideout

For the second time, Lucy Tallwoman honked her horn at Harley Ponyboy's old trailer but still no one came to the door, or even peeked out the window, as far as she could tell. She could see Harley's truck was gone, but he sometimes loaned it to one of the neighbors to haul something or other. He might yet be in there. After honking again, then waiting a rea- sonable amount of time, she at last decided Harley was gone for sure and reluctantly lifted a covered dish from the seat beside her, and then headed for the trailer's rickety old porch. She deposited the bowl of lamb stew on the top step. Harley no longer had a dog so it should be okay there, she thought. It was moving on toward evening and he should be home soon, regardless—he hadn't been drinking for a while now, and didn't spend any more time in town than he had to, according to her husband. Lucy got back in her truck, still worried something might happen to the stew, and after sitting there a moment thought she should go back and set the food just inside the door...just in case. It occurred to her one of the neighbor's dogs might come along; a dog could smell lamb stew a good distance. In the end, however, she decided it was an unnecessary bother and pointed the truck back down the ruts to the highway and home.

Just as Lucy Tallwoman reached the last rise before the big road, she happened to glance in her side mirror, and despite the dust, could have sworn the container of stew was no longer on Harley's front step. It was getting dark and she thought she might be mistaken. She certainly wasn't going to drive back up there just to check. Her family was waiting for *their* bowl of stew.

That night, around the table, Lucy said she had been to visit a sick clan member that morning, and on the way back, dropped off a little something for Harley Ponyboy as well. He wasn't home, she said, but mentioned she intended to sit him down and talk to him again about that woman with the good job; the one who was thinking of taking another husband. The woman told Lucy she found being single not to her liking after all. The fact that she already knew Harley, and had even mentioned him in a favorable light, was a pure stroke of luck to Lucy's way of thinking. "That sort of thing won't be happening for you every day," she meant to tell him should she get the chance.

No one had seen Harley for a while now and Thomas, earlier, had mentioned it was beginning to worry him. "Harley don't eat right when he's out there by himself," he said.

Old Man Paul T'Sosi wondered, but to no one in particular, if Harley might not need the services of a *hataalii* such as himself? To his recollection it had been over a year since Harley's last cleansing ceremony. Paul kept his patients' records in his head, and

45

since there were not that many, he was seldom wrong. "Maybe he's having the urge to get drunk…or maybe he already is." He looked pointedly at his son-in-law. "You know a man might need a little help from time to time, to stay on the wagon."

Thomas sighed, and cautiously allowed there was that possibility. *Harley might have stumbled.* "I guess we could take a run by there tomorrow and check on him. I did tell him last week I might have time to help him on his trailer this weekend."

Lucy Tallwoman raised her eyebrows at this, "I thought we were going into Farmington tomorrow?"

Thomas looked surprised. "Hmm, well, to be honest, I guess I'd forgotten about that."

His wife frowned and looked at her father. "And you are going with him in the morning? I thought you were going to go with the sheep so the kids could get caught up with their homework?"

Young Caleb Begay perked up his ears at this new possibility. Any chance to avoid homework was always at the top of his agenda. "I don't mind going with the sheep in the morning. Ida Marie and I can easy take those sheep by ourselves."

His older sister puffed up. "You speak for your-self, little man. I've got to get caught up on some of that school stuff…and so do you."

Lucy looked from the children to her husband. "So what's it going to be? It's starting to look like I'll be taking the sheep. Then who's going to help the kids with their homework, huh?"

Lucy was beginning to cloud up, and Thomas knew that was not a good sign. He glanced around the table, and ran everything around in his head for a

46

moment, but still couldn't come up with anything he thought might satisfy her.

Paul T'Sosi shook his head. "I'll take the damn sheep. You and Lucy can run by Harley's place and check on him, and then maybe go on into town together."

Ida Marie spoke up, shaking her head at the adults, when she said, "I can help Caleb with his homework. I don't need any help with mine. I just have some reading for history class on Monday."

Lucy shot Thomas a quick glance, and was about to say something harsh, when she suddenly brightened. "I'll call Sue Yazzie to run into town with me. Thomas can go help Harley for a while then come back to check on the kids." She looked pleased at so obvious a solution and glanced around the table, as though daring anyone to come up with a better idea, but of course, no one could.

Not one of them suspected her plan would turn out as it did.

5

The Searcher

Charlie Yazzie had barely finished feeding the horses, and was still filling their water tank when he heard the neighbor's guinea hens screeching. He looked up to see a Navajo Police unit making its way up the gravel drive—straight into a gaggle of the alarmed fowl. The birds were good watchdogs but they were beginning to get on Charlie's nerves. His wife, Sue, liked to watch them and said they picked every bug out of the garden—yet left the tomatoes untouched. She now considered the birds her allies and was increasingly protective of the raucous fowl. Little Joseph Wiley liked to chase them, but they occasionally turned tables, and chased *him* instead. Several times the boy's pup had to come to his rescue.

As the police unit came closer, Charlie could see Billy Red Clay silently cussing the guineas while doing his best not to run any over. When the policeman finally pulled up to the corrals, Charlie could see his mouth still working—cursing under his breath.

Charlie was laughing as he called, "What's up Officer...don't like guineas?"

One male bird, bolder than the others, chose this moment to charge the policeman and Billy had to kick at it to change its mind. "Why in the hell would anyone put up with these things?"

"People say they're good eating...if you can catch one...which I haven't seen anyone do yet. And they hide their eggs out, so they're no good for that either."

Billy patted his sidearm, "I'll bet I could catch a few." He grinned. "Have you eaten any of 'em yourself?"

"No, but I would if I thought I could get away with it. My son can't go out in the yard without the dog and they're running *him* ragged."

Billy leaned on the corral to watch silently as the horse tank filled, almost to the brim, before Charlie shut it off; then the policeman remembered the reason for his visit. "I thought you might be interested in what's going on with the Benny Klee investigation. I haven't heard from the Feds as yet this morning, but our boys have been poking around a little. Hastiin Sosi was out to the old man's place yesterday to break the news to his wife. When she finally calmed down, she claimed her husband had quite a lot of money with him. She told Hastiin he was going into Farmington to trade trucks and intended to finish the deal with cash to avoid any more payments. She said he'd been saving up for a long time. Hastiin had to tell her no money was found on her husband, or in the truck. He said she was some disappointed to hear that. Then later she asked if the old man's gun had been found in the truck? He didn't always take it with him, she said, but since he was carrying so much cash she thought he might have." Billy went on talking before Charlie could ask. "Dudd Schott's boys didn't find any gun. Not that I could see in any of the reports anyway."

"She didn't say how much money he had with him, did she?"

"No. I guess the old man was pretty tight lipped with her when it came to his money. He was a silversmith and apparently doing pretty well with it these last few years. The old man just told her it was time he had a newer truck and that he could afford it." Billy frowned. "The wife said he left the house by himself. He asked his youngest son to go with him earlier in the week, she said, but the boy thought it might take his father most of the day to find a truck he liked and just didn't have time for it. He works in the mines up there somewhere. The officer looked down and scuffed the dirt with the toe of his boot. "I'll bet he wishes he'd gone along now."

"So, you figure Benny picked up someone along the way? Someone he knew…or a hitchhiker maybe?"

"Could be. We're going to give it to the media this afternoon…see if maybe someone was spotted hitching around there yesterday morning." Billy's voice trailed off as he watched Sue's mare wring her tail and charge up to the water tank to nip Charlie's gelding on the rear end. She ran him off and then drank her fill. "She in season?" Billy thought the mare was.

"Beats me." The investigator shrugged, then grinned. "She's always been a little mean with other horses. She's good with Sue, though, that's all I care about." Charlie turned down the water and started the hose down the little ditch to the peach trees.

Billy looked the trees over with a critical eye. "I remember when you planted those... I believe they will make you some peaches this year." He sounded almost jealous at the thought of it. He liked peaches and his own few trees had done poorly the previous season.

Charlie looked down the short row of trees and nodded agreement. "Already had a few last year...and they were covered with blossoms this spring. You might be right."

Peaches and apricots were some of the first fruit trees the Navajo learned to grow and some of the few that would grow in the harsher conditions on the reservation. The fact that the fruit could be dried and would last the winter was a major advantage.

"Sue thinks she'll have enough to can this fall." Charlie's forebears originally took to the fruit because they could be grown along the washes taking advantage of runoff. Some varieties were able to survive with very little care: an important consideration when a family had to be off to the higher pastures all summer, at times, staying away from home until the corn ripened in the fall. A few families might occasionally send boys back to weed corn, and ditch around the trees. But, as often as not, that didn't happen and the trees had to fend for themselves.

When Kit Carson's Ute scouts brought soldiers against the Navajo in 1864; the fruit trees, cornfields, and those boys, were first to suffer the government's wrath...and the ensuing scorched earth policy that followed. Consequently, those trees were some of the first things the government helped replace when the people returned after the Long Walk.

"Anything else, Billy...or you came all the way out here just to keep me in the loop?" Charlie smiled as he said this, but not long enough for Billy to catch it.

Billy Red Clay grinned, "Not really. I was on my way into the Sheriff's Office in Farmington anyway, and being's how I had to go right by here, I thought I might as well stop in."

"Sheriff's Office? Not to see Dudd Schott I hope?" Charlie Yazzie had long been at odds with the new sheriff and didn't hesitate to say so. He knew Billy didn't care for the man either. As a deputy, Schott had constantly harassed those Indians he thought he could intimidate and made many of their visits to town unpleasant, to say the least. The deputy's later election to the office of sheriff had shocked everyone, including Dudd, who put his name on the ballot mostly at the insistence of his wife who had family in high places. There were apparently enough people who didn't know him to allow him to be elected.

"Yep, I'm off to see the High Sheriff himself," Billy joked. He knew most everyone on the reservation felt the same as he and Charlie Yazzie did when it came to Dudd Schott, and so didn't bother to belabor the point. It did, however, lead him to the real reason for his visit. "Apparently some indigent was found dead up in Farmington this morning. Navajo, they think, so they notified us. They're calling it a probable 'natural causes' and the FBI has already been there, done their little forensic dance, and left.

The sheriff's office has a copy of the preliminary for Tribal and, of course, they wanted *us* to notify next of kin. The dead man might be anyone from anywhere. All they know is, he's an Indian. They haven't been able to pull up anything on him as yet." Billy made a noise in his throat, "That doesn't surprise me one damn bit either. We'll have to wait for the FBI to update us on this one...probably first thing in the morning. The remains are going in for autopsy sometime in the next few hours."

Charlie showed less interest in this new case than Billy had hoped, and after a few more minutes of small talk, Officer Red Clay said his goodbyes: waving a final farewell from his vehicle as he pulled out––this time, vigorously honking his horn at the collection of guineas who had gathered to peck at their reflection in the unit's shiny hubcaps.

As Charlie stood in the early morning sun he listened to the muted roar of the river across the highway—the San Juan—gathering itself after taking on the clear cold waters of the *Rio de Los Animas Perdidas*—The River of Lost Souls: an appropriate name, Charlie thought, for a river flowing from the upper canyons of the earliest Anasazi.

The investigator's thoughts turned again to the untimely end of the old silversmith from Teec Nos Pos. Now there was something else nibbling at him, and when it finally came to him hours later, he was appalled; he knew then what he must do.

6

The Autopsy

Billy Red Clay only waited on the bench outside Sheriff Dudd Schott's office long enough for boredom to set in—then decided a coffee might help. He had seen a breakroom just up the hall as he entered and thought he might slip in for a quick cup. He'd be back before anyone noticed.

The room was empty except for two young deputies at a back table; the pair appeared to be deep in discussion and paid him little mind.

As Billy doctored his coffee he couldn't help overhearing the deputy with his back to him, say, "They've been in there over an hour now. I should be out on patrol already, but the Sheriff left word for me to see him in his office. He wants me to take some Navajo cop to look at a body." His companion nudged him and raised an eyebrow in the direction of Billy Red Clay.

The Navajo policeman didn't look their way or offer any sign he'd overheard. He left concentrating on stirring his coffee. *Why in the hell would Dudd Schott want me to see the body; do they think I can verify he was a Navajo? As though someone can tell by looking.*

Billy was back on the bench and nearly finished with his coffee when an older, officious-looking sheriff's officer opened the door and beckoned him in, motioning for him to bring his coffee along with him. It wasn't Dudd Schott and the young Navajo policeman was pleased to see it; he couldn't help considering it a stroke of good luck.

The older deputy put out a hand and Billy shook it. "Sorry about the wait." The deputy moved around to the big leather chair behind the desk after motioning Billy to a plainer wooden one in front.

"Officer Red Clay, is it?" The older deputy was looking at a set of papers. Billy guessed they were the FBI report from the investigation of the indigent's death. "Sheriff Schott was called to a Commissioners' meeting this morning and regrets he missed you." He paused and looked at Billy, seemed to assess the young Navajo, but not in the judgmental way Billy was used to seeing from white lawmen. "I'm Under Sheriff Bob Danforth. The sheriff asked me to sit in for him this morning and asks your indulgence in having a look at the victim's body. It seems the man had some unusual tattoos. The FBI thought they might have some tribal significance and hoped you might be able to help us out." The undersheriff tapped the stack of papers. "We understand you are the new FBI Liaison Officer for Tribal and already know Federal Agent Smith, who by the way, will be meeting us there. There's a deputy standing by to ferry us over there as we speak but only if you have time of course."

Billy Red Clay toyed with the thought of saying "No, I actually don't have time...not after waiting outside a good portion of the morning." But he had not become liaison officer by turning down FBI requests. And this Undersheriff seemed a cut above the pompous Dudd Schott. "I'd be happy to help anyway I can—though I'm not sure how much I'll be able to tell you about any tattoos."

"Well, we'd appreciate any input you might have to offer."

The young deputy, the one Billy had overheard in the break room, was waiting just outside the door. The Deputy was red-faced, and unable to meet the tribal policeman's gaze, as he led them to a back entrance and a waiting patrol car.

~~~~~~~

Later in the afternoon, on his way back to Shiprock, Billy Red Clay felt sick—part of which he attributed to the morbidity of the autopsy—and partly to the discovery of the dead man's identity which the FBI had figured out well before he got there. Billy, at first, did not recognize the man by name, though he later realized they were related. Nez was quite a common name on the reservation. The connection only clicked into place when he studied the person's face—usually so different in death—not with this clan uncle who looked remarkably like he had in life, possibly even younger, as though the stress of living had been lifted from him.

Gilbert Nez was known to have been in town only days earlier, asking after various family members, mainly his wife, who had now been dead for seven or eight years. She was Thomas's mother, Billy's great aunt, who wound up in a mental facility toward the end. Thomas blamed that on his father, too. Now Gilbert was dead and it turned out he'd only wanted money, according to talk.

The medical examiner pointed out a small series of numbers tattooed on the man's arm. "As it turns out," he said, "it's the man's Social Security number which led to the identification of the body." The doctor gazed thoughtfully at the tattoo. "It's something a man who leads a reckless life might do, perhaps to ensure his remains make their way back home."

That made sense to Billy Red Clay. Where a person was born and grew up was important to a *Diné*. It was where their umbilical cord was buried, and where some thought they should end up when everything was said and done. No matter how far away life might take them, most Navajo have the hope they will, someday, return to the *Dinétah*, if only in death.

The doctor went on about the numbers, saying, "Social Security, should you younger men not be aware, was instituted in the waning days of the Great Depression when hope, and money, was still in short supply." He scratched his head and said he hadn't seen such a tattoo in many years—and never on a Navajo.

According to the coroner, men who 'rode the rails' or otherwise associated themselves with chancy occupations sometimes employed the practice as a safeguard against winding up in a potter's field somewhere. "Back in those days such people often didn't live to sixty-five—not long enough for them to receive regular benefits." The doctor chuckled, "This may have been the only good some of them ever realized from the program."

When Billy Red Clay made himself look more closely at the deceased's tattoos he saw only the typical jailhouse art—common to a man who led this sort of life. A few of the tattoos might possibly be of a cultural nature, he thought, but he was unable to say what significance they might actually have. There was one he thought might represent the Salt People, mostly because he knew Gilbert Nez was of that clan. There was yet another of what he took to be Navajo Mountain; a holy place where a great many of the Salt Clan have lived for the last hundred years or so. Billy knew the images, crude as they might be, were part of Gilbert's personal power—or 'medicine,' and not to be discussed with *billiganna*. White people didn't understand this kind of medicine...or what it might mean to a *Diné*. *There are people who might know what all these symbols are,* he thought to himself, *but none of those people would ever tell.*

Eventually, the other law enforcement personnel, including Agent Fred Smith, left the autopsy room. Billy Red Clay stayed behind and when the medical examiner followed the others out for a last word; Billy had a chance to look a final time upon his great-uncle. The leathery left hand showed those particular disfigurements associated with a horseman—one who makes his living with a rope—more common in later years when an almost imperceptible decline in ability may catch him unaware. An appendage might be caught in a dally between rope and horn, to be lost forever. The first joint of Gilbert Nez's thumb and index finger were missing—bearing mute testimony to the fading of a man's reflexes—as life and luck run their inevitable course.

~~~~~~

On his way back to Shiprock, Billy Red Clay was nearly to the Yazzie's turnoff, when it suddenly occurred to him he should again touch base with the tribal investigator before making the depressing trip out to see his Uncle Thomas. Maybe Charlie would go with him to break the news. That might make it some easier—knowing full well *there is no easy way to tell a man his father is dead.*

Even before Billy was out of the car, Charlie appeared at the door with his keys in his hand, seemingly surprised to see the policeman back so soon.

"I was just on my way to see you," the investigator said. "Dispatch let me know you were on your way back to headquarters." The pair stood on the front porch, each man with hat in hand, as Billy filled the investigator in on his interagency meeting in Farmington, finally getting around to the autopsy of Gilbert Nez.

Charlie shook his head. "After you left this morning it occurred to me that might be who it was." He saw confusion cross the policeman's face at this and hesitated a moment to gather his thoughts before continuing. "Your Uncle Thomas and I were in Farmington last night, Billy. He ran into Gilbert at the Social Club, purely accidental…he hadn't seen the man in thirty years…hadn't heard from him at all in fact." Charlie went on to tell Billy everything that took place at Rosie's and then admitted, "I called Thomas after you left this morning and told him what I suspected—I told him I would run by your office and see what the autopsy report had to say." Charlie threw up his hands. "That's where I was heading when you showed up."

Charlie hesitated once more. "Thomas said he was just leaving for Harley Ponyboy's place to check on him but said he would hold off until I got back to him about Gilbert...one way or the other."

Billy Red Clay gave the investigator another strange look, and the irritation in his voice was clear when he asked, "What in hell were you and my Uncle Thomas doing at Rosie's last night? Poking around in the Benny Klee case? The FBI, and by that I mean Agent Smith, will be very disappointed to hear you two were digging around in this thing." Billy turned and looked out across Sue's garden; the guineas were nowhere in sight. "I was hoping we could get off on a better footing with the Bureau this time around and now this!" The officer rubbed the back of his neck, "This isn't good Charlie... this is not good at all." The young officer sounded just like Samuel Shorthair when he said. "You are going to have to stay out of it. It isn't your jurisdiction and damned sure not your investigation."

Charlie, somewhat embarrassed, shifted from one foot to the other but looked directly at the Tribal officer when he finally agreed. "You are absolutely right, Billy, we shouldn't have gone. I'm the one who talked Thomas into it; he only went to help me out. But it's done and there's no fixing it now. If you want, I can go on out to Thomas's and let him know about his father. I had planned on that anyway. Thomas might take it better from me than anyone else...even a nephew." He looked straight at the officer. "Your Uncle Thomas tries to let on he didn't care about his father...but he did...and he feels guilty about leaving him down there last night; it was written all over him when he dropped me off." Charlie canted his head slightly, "Do they know what killed Gilbert Nez?"

Billy sighed, "Not yet. The medical examiner thinks maybe natural causes. So that's all anyone knows until they get the lab results back."

Billy Red Clay was not yet ready to let go of Charlie's meddling and went steely-eyed as he continued. "I'm not going to say anything about this just yet and just hope the bureau doesn't get wind of it. From what you say, Rosie never saw *you* and the only other witness is dead now. Hopefully this will be it." Billy stopped for a moment and thought about Charlie's offer. "Maybe it would be best if you went out to Uncle Thomas's place. I've blown my entire day in town and still have stacks of stuff on my desk; some of it has to go out this afternoon. And you're probably closer to him than I am. I'll catch up with you later and see how it went." And with that, Officer Red Clay, still visibly upset, stomped down to his vehicle and drove off—secretly hoping to catch a guinea hen crossing the road.

Charlie stood watching the policeman go and for the first time felt the full burden of what he'd done—especially for the involvement of Thomas Begay. Neither of them had broken any law but protocol had been abused and that might be even harder to fix. This was the second time in two days Billy Red Clay had been right and he had been in the wrong. *Am I slipping?* he wondered to himself. *Maybe I'm not doing any of this just to be helpful. Maybe I'm starting to believe in all the hype. Charlie Yazzie… 'Investigator'.*

~~~~~~

When he eased up the rain-rutted track to Thomas Begay's, Charlie had already reconciled himself to the fact that his involvement in the Klee murder investigation was less than proper, but he still wasn't sure it had been harmful. He still might be able to offer insight by virtue of legal experience. But even *that* would not justify crossing the lines of jurisdiction.

As the Investigator stepped out of his truck he saw Ida Marie Begay and her brother Caleb, peering out the kitchen window of Lucy Tallwoman's new house. The pair thought the sound of the truck to be their stepmother returning from town. Still they were not disappointed to see Charlie Yazzie instead; the investigator had gone to great lengths in the interests of both of them over the years and they had developed close ties to him and his family.

Charlie stood, seemingly perplexed, one hand still on the door handle of the truck, as he mulled over what he had come to tell his friend. It was then Thomas's father-in-law, old man T'Sosi, came from the direction of the family hogan now eclipsed by the newer structure. The old singer lived out there alone now which was how he preferred it. He took his meals at his daughter's table but spent less and less time with the family.

Charlie waited for the old man to approach. Paul's hearing was failing and should he call a greeting now he would only have to repeat it when Paul drew nearer.

Paul T'Sosi had the dust of the corrals on him and took off his hat to hit it against his leg leaving a small greenish cloud on the evening air. The old man smiled at his visitor but skipped the greetings. "What brings a Tribal man out this way?" He gestured over his shoulder at the sheep milling in the holding pen. "I brought them in a little early today. Thomas has to do some doctoring on the lambs. Two have infections where he docked their tails last week." He raised a finger and shook it. "I told him we should just let them keep their tails; it's how we have always done it. But he's been talking to the county agent again—and that one thinks this new way is best." The old man smiled grimly. "Now, maybe Thomas will admit I was right." Paul and his daughter's husband were in constant disagreement since the county agent began dropping by with his fresh new ideas and devious ways to change things. Paul had done those things a certain way for more than half a century; it made no sense to change now.

Charlie pulled a face, and nodded along with him, knowing later he would have to agree with Thomas Begay as well, and on the same complaint, but the other side.

Thomas himself soon interrupted the men's talk, calling a greeting on his way up from the pens. "What took you so long...did you hear something from Billy?" Thomas was wiping the remnants of a greasy ointment on his jeans, almost smiling, until he was close enough to see the expression on Charlie's face. He knew the look.

"Bad news?"

"Yes, it's about Gilbert."

A cloud fell across Thomas's features and he grew instantly serious; he hadn't heard anyone call his father Gilbert in a long time.

Paul T'Sosi, too, was now frowning and moved closer so as not to miss anything. He wasn't sure yet who Charlie was talking about but could see Thomas did, and if the news affected his son-in-law it affected them all. A Navajo family keeps few secrets from one another, and considers everyone's input equally important, even on the slightest issues.

Thomas instantly thought it could only be one of two things: either his father was in jail...or he was dead. From Charlie's face, he took it to be the latter. "Dead?" he asked calmly.

Charlie nodded, "Last night from what they figure...probably just after we left him."

Thomas nodded. "What happened?"

"Natural causes, they think, but the lab reports aren't back yet so the coroner won't sign off on an official certificate until he sees the reports."

Thomas's face fell and he turned away for a moment, but when he turned back and looked at Charlie, there was no sign of regret or sadness. He had long ago given up any thought of reconciliation with his father, and after his mother died, he gradually relinquished any feelings for the man. Charlie knew this was Thomas Begay's way of dealing with his father's death—that is to say, not dealing with it all.

Charlie had seen this many times in his work for Legal Services. He knew a Navajo family will stand by an *'Adláanii,* sometimes for many years and through unspeakable incidents of drunken violence or other even more regrettable behavior—trying again and again to bring them back to the true path. They willingly pay for ceremonies or detox treatment time after time—even holding private family interventions—until, finally, when the person does something so unconscionable it can no longer be put up with, he is let go. Then he is *yóó'a'háás'Kaah* or 'one who is lost,' not only to his relatives but to all the people...and that can mean forever. It generally takes one of only a select few offenses to become a lost one—a woman abandoning a child, or incest, or murder all cardinal sins in the way of the Navajo.

Paul T'Sosi rubbed his jaw, and looked away. News of a death is serious business for a *hataalii,* and he thought it time they held a ceremony for Thomas Begay to help him with this loss. He knew his son-in-law wouldn't be up for it just yet, so backed away and didn't say anything. He decided to wait, speak to his daughter about it...see what she thought. *A variation of a Blessing Way might do it or maybe even a Ghost Way chant, should the type be carefully chosen.* He could handle most of it himself so it wouldn't cost the family much more than food for the guests, and possibly a *dry* painter, as the old people called sand painting. Paul, himself, knew how to make the paintings, but had grown tremulous of late, and now left it to younger men with steadier hands.

Thomas, seeing the old man's face and knowing the signs, quickly changed the subject and began talking about Harley Ponyboy, saying, "Lucy saw Alfred Nakii at the Co-op in Shiprock yesterday." The hint of a smile came to his lips. "When she asked him if he'd seen Harley Ponyboy, he told her he thinks Harley might have a new girlfriend—he thinks that may be the reason we haven't heard much from him. He wouldn't say much more about it; you know Alfred, he don't say a whole helluva lot." He shook his head at the others. "I asked him once why he ate that burro he stole that time. He just said, 'I was getting hungry,' and walked off without another word." All three men smiled at this…already knowing how Alfred was. Thomas nodded at the others, "This is Sunday. Harley told us last week he would drop by for supper tonight. If he doesn't, I'm going out there in the morning and see what's what." Thomas looked annoyed. "I wish he had a phone. They've been saying they'll have the lines out there in a few more months." He smiled. "I'm not sure Harley will sign up for service anyway. I'm starting to think he likes being alone out there. He's going to wind up being a damned little hermit."

Old man Paul T'Sosi judged the sun as it slid toward the hogback. "If Lucy doesn't get back from town pretty quick there may not be any supper anyway."

7

Diyin Dine'é

Harley Ponyboy, on his drive back from Shiprock, with his barrels of water sloshing around in the back of the truck, eyed his meager supply of groceries in the cardboard box beside him. He couldn't help but feel he was on the verge of a new chapter in his life. There were stirrings—not just in regard to Eileen Smith—but rather some otherworldly premonition that his life was about to change. The *Diyin Dine'é,* the Holy People, shrouded in their invisible aura, were near. He was sure of it now. It would bring a change for the better, he was certain. This was something Harley had never experienced before: the old people spoke of it...saying the Holy People came to everyone sooner or later. This must be his time.

Harley realized his mental state suffered after Anita was gone, leaving him feeling guilty, responsible even, and unable to fathom why.

No, this was a matter of *hosoji*—or rather the lack of it—a fundamental illness of spirit which dogged him since Anita's death. Now there was this almost palpable awareness of impending hope—a second chance—*maybe the Holy People think I have suffered enough.* He was determined not to waste such a gift.

As Harley pointed the truck up the rough track to the trailer—being careful not to upset the water barrels—he wondered if Eileen Smith (if that truly was her name) would still be there. He knew he was naïve in some ways, yet thought himself reasonably perceptive in others. "I may be ignorant," he sometimes told himself, "but I am not stupid." What intentions Eileen might have escaped him, but he was certain they included more than selling him a Bible. The woman had passed up the opportunity for a trip to town and it was obvious, even for one of his slight experience, that she might have reason not to leave; some reason beyond what she had first intimated. She might feel the need to keep a low profile for some reason. He had, from the start, suspected the woman needed help; what that help might require never entered his mind. Through all these doubts and suppositions, Harley Ponyboy remained determined to help the troubled woman regardless of consequence.

Harley barely had time to shut off the engine before the trailer door opened a crack. He couldn't help giving a sigh of relief at the sight of Eileen. Peeping out, and seeing it was him, she came to help with whatever he brought from town. He immediately noticed her hair, not styled in any particular fashion and with a natural wave falling clean and shimmering almost to her waist. It seemed even brighter in the afternoon sun and had a bounce to it just as his shampoo bottle promised.

"Eileen, if you'll take this box of food in," he said, handing her the cardboard container, "I'll take the truck around and pump these barrels into the tank. I don't like to leave that kind of weight on the springs; it makes them sag. They're old and might not come back one of these times."

Eileen only nodded and took the groceries, then watched from the window as he pulled the truck behind the trailer-house. *Good,* she thought, *maybe he will leave it back there out of sight; it might help people think no one's home.* She was thinking of the woman who came by earlier to leave the container of stew on the front steps. Eileen was lucky to hear the pickup coming up the grade giving her time to lock the door and hide. She wondered if it was a sister of Harley's or maybe a girlfriend or...well, she had not thought him the sort to attract the attention of females. Granted, there was a certain down-to-earth charm, even a sense of honesty, about him. She learned long ago that looks weren't everything when it came to men—or women, either, as far as that went. This Harley Ponyboy was certainly no great prize should he be judged by looks alone.

Harley came into the house wet—water still dripping from his hair. "Hose got away from me!" he laughed. "It's a big pump...puts out more pressure than you might think."

Eileen had no idea how much pressure such a pump might have but nodded agreeably as she put away the groceries. "A woman came by this afternoon and left a bowl of something on the steps. I put it in the icebox. It smelled pretty good. Do you want to have that for supper?"

Harley stopped mopping the water from his face and turned to look at her before answering. It was an unnecessary consideration in so small a space, but he liked to look at her...and he liked that she called the refrigerator an icebox, just as he did, despite being corrected by nearly everyone.

"You didn't answer the door?"

"No. I must have been using the hairdryer and didn't hear her," she lied. "I peeked out as she was going down the road and noticed she'd left something." And, again, she asked, "It's a stew, I think. You want to have that stew for supper?"

"Uh...sure. That would be fine. Some people were making fresh fry bread outside the store so I picked some up. It would go good with stew, if that is what it is. We'd best eat it tonight anyway; fry bread is never as good the next day...but you probably know that." Harley paused and put the towel down. "Did you see what sort of vehicle she was driving?"

"I just caught a glimpse of it before it went over the hill...green...it was a green pickup, I think. It could have been a Ford."

Harley thought for only a second then nodded. "That would be Lucy Tallwoman's truck. She's a weaver; I expect you'd like her."

"Old friend?" Eileen smiled when she asked this, but Harley thought he detected a note of worry, which somehow pleased him.

"She is my best friend's wife, but sure, she's an old friend, too. She and Thomas Begay now have Thomas's two kids, and her father, living with them. They are all good people, but for some damn reason they think I don't eat enough." Harley laughed and rubbed his belly. "They are wrong as you can plainly see." The little man turned thoughtful, "It's funny how people always think a single man is not able to cook for himself." He turned to the radio and clicked on KTNN. "It'll be time for the news in a few minutes—there's a story I've been following about an old man who got murdered up on 64. It happened yesterday morning. Whoever killed him stole his truck, too." He clucked to himself and adjusted the frequency. "I swear I don't know what the world's coming to. Seems like you can't trust anyone nowadays." He was about to modify the statement in deference to Eileen, when the intro for the five o'clock news blared and he hurried to lower the volume. He helped set the table only half-listening to the few national stories the station felt their listeners might find interesting.

Eileen was heating the stew but glanced at the radio a time or two before saying, "Would you mind just turning that thing off, Harley?"

"Oh, I will in just a minute. It's just that I might be related to that old man. I'm *of* the Reed People Clan if I didn't mention it before." He hesitated. "And *for* the Near-to-Water Clan on the other side." Then smiled shyly. "You never said what clan you are, Eileen?"

Eileen considered the question, sniffed, and said, "I'm from an Irish clan on my father's side but my mother never told me what clan she was. My Aunt Mary said she wanted to get away from such things and wanted me to do the same. 'Your mother says white people don't enquire what 'clan' everyone is when they meet. So why should we?"

71

Harley stood up straighter and raised his chin slightly. "Well, you know, Eileen, such as that can be important out here. There's really not that many of us and getting paired up wrong can put everyone in danger."

"Is that so? What kind of danger are we talking about Harley? What? A boogeyman might get us if we are from the same clan?"

"No, Eileen, I don't think a boogeyman might get us. But it's the *Diné* way that people of the same clan should not get together—if you know what I mean. My boss, Professor Custer, says it probably came about way back in our past to avoid inbreeding and such. There were a lot fewer of us back then and we had to be even more careful of that sort of thing." Harley looked out the window a moment. "We Navajo think it's just something the Holy People want us to be careful about, that's all. It's part of our religion."

"I thought you weren't religious Harley."

"I am in some ways—the old ways."

Eileen stirred the stew so hard a little of it slopped over the edge of the pan. "The thing is, Harley, we're not 'getting together' so I wouldn't worry too much what clan we are."

Harley Ponyboy frowned as he put the butter on the table. "Why I never expected anything of the sort Eileen." Which was not strictly true and they both knew it. He would have denied it further but realized the radio newsman was already into the local stories and talking about the murder up on 64.

The announcer was young and had a good voice even if his Navajo was not perfect. "The man's name, released only hours ago, is Benny Klee, a silversmith from the area just east of Teec Nos Pos. The elderly man was reportedly on his way into Farmington, New Mexico to purchase a truck, when he was apparently lured to the side of the road and murdered. Details are still sketchy but authorities say his vehicle has been located, undamaged, and is undergoing forensic examination by the local office of the FBI. A spokesman told KTNN news there are few leads in the killing but went on to assure us an intensive investigation is underway. The FBI urges anyone on the reservation with information regarding the crime to come forward."

When Harley turned back to the table, Eileen was staring at the radio, slightly pale, and with a set to her jaw.

Harley immediately reassured her, "Don't worry, Eileen, that's a long way from here. But it does point up the fact that a person shouldn't be out on the roads hitchhiking. It's something you should really think about in the future."

Eileen did her best to regain her composure then looked sideways at Harley, a questioning glance that carried the implication he might have a screw loose. "So," she muttered, moving to the stove to fill their bowls. "Was the old man on the news a relation or not?"

"Not that I'm aware of, right now. But I do have a lot of clan up that way and most of them are older people." He snorted, "The FBI urges people with information to come forward." He laughed outright. "No one on the reservation ever comes forward. We have more murders—and less convictions—than most big cities. At least that's what Charlie Yazzie says."

"And how would this Charlie Yazzie know that?" Eileen was curious.

"Oh, Charlie is a lawyer and Legal Service's Investigator. He knows a lot about crime, especially here on the reservation."

The woman pursed her lips and a shadow fell across her features. "He's a cop?"

Harley chuckled. "That's what everyone thinks. No, he's not a cop. He's more like a social worker, I guess. He does carry a badge, though, and is licensed to carry a gun…when he remembers it."

He unwrapped the fry bread and put it on the table then took the bowl of stew she handed him. When he looked across he said, "This stew does smell good, Eileen, I think it's that recipe Lucy has been working on; she got it from Marissa, a white woman living with Thomas's Uncle Johnny Nez up at Navajo Mountain."

"She's a white woman living with a Navajo?"

Harley could see her working this over in her mind. "Marissa is an anthropologist—some people think that makes it all right."

"I never said it wasn't right. I've just never heard of a white woman and a Navajo man living together––I doubt it would happen where I come from."

"Where's that?"

"Salt Lake…well, a little south of there."

"You said your father was white." Harley was having a hard time seeing a distinction in the case of John Nez.

Eileen thought about it and couldn't come up with much of an answer. "I don't know; it just seems different that's all."

"Well, like I said, they're married and those people up at Navajo Mountain seem to think it's all right. They elected him to the Tribal Council a couple of years back." Harley took another bite of the stew and smacked his lips. "Yes, I think Lucy may have finally got that recipe down."

~~~~~~

The next morning, when Harley Ponyboy finally pulled himself out of bed, he was surprised to hear someone in the kitchen and had to think a minute before it came to him who it was. He smiled when he smelled bacon frying. It had been a long time since he awoke to so pleasant a morning and he savored it as he dressed and washed up for breakfast—which proved to be both a leisurely and pleasant affair.

Harley considered the conversation 'stimulating' as Professor Custer sometimes called such agreeable talks; he felt reasonably sure he had held up his end.

Eileen said she hoped it didn't get as hot there as it did down in Phoenix. "I've seen it 120 degrees down there and for days at a time, too. But it's the humidity...people don't realize how much moisture those truck farms and swimming pools put into the air."

Harley tried to look surprised, though he had, himself, worked one summer on those farms and was well aware of the heat and humidity in that country. "Well, you won't see that up here, Eileen. I would be surprised if it gets much over ninety here today…and that's with a humidity well under fourteen percent." Harley had worked closely with Professor Custer for the last several years and thought he had learned something about the proper way to couch certain day-to-day comments on the weather—always a popular topic of conversation.

"So, no swamp cooler?" Eileen couldn't imagine living without air conditioning. "I thought I noticed one up on the roof. I would think they would work pretty good up in this dry country."

"Yep, there's one up there, like new, too—never been used that I know of. It would probably work great if I could keep it in water. You'd be surprised how much water they use up on a hot day." Harley made a mental note to pick up some more water barrels next time he could afford them. He was sure Eileen Smith would enjoy that cooler on some of the warmer days.

Eileen just started clearing the table and running water for dishes when Harley Ponyboy cocked his head to one side, listened, and then looked toward the highway.

Eileen, noticing this, shut off the water and said, "What?"

"I believe someone's coming up the road from the highway—and I think I know who it is." The sound of Thomas's diesel truck was unmistakable, even more so, since the muffler had fallen off. A lot of vehicles on the reservation were without mufflers. It's hard to keep a muffler intact when you're high centering all the time. Thomas thought it sounded good that way and had decided not to replace it unless he got stopped—not likely on the reservation—but he had to be careful in Farmington.

Eileen ran to the window in the front bedroom and peered from behind a curtain. "There's someone coming all right!" she sounded a little distraught and called to him, "Don't tell anyone I'm here Harley. Go outside to talk to them."

Harley walked over to the little round window in the door and sighed. It was Thomas Begay and he was by himself. He would expect to come in and have coffee at the least. Harley glanced toward the front bedroom just as Eileen slammed the door, and he heard the lock click. The lock on that particular door didn't work but he doubted Eileen knew that. He sighed, hitched up his pants, and walked out to greet his visitor—catching Thomas by surprise.

Thomas's first words were terse, "Where you been, Shorty?"

When Thomas called him Shorty, Harley knew his friend had his back up about something and might be hard to deal with. This wasn't going to be easy.

"I have been right here," the little man smiled. "I jus' been working on the place."

Thomas looked around. "Everything looks about the same to me. You must not be making much progress."

"I been working inside painting, if you must know." Harley kept whatever trepidation Eileen had engendered out of his voice and broke into a grin. "So, what brings you out here this morning big boy, and why so damn grumpy."

"Grumpy? I'm not grumpy. I'm pissed. Where were you last night? You were supposed to come by for supper, if you'll recall. Lucy had a big meal fixed and when you didn't show she packaged up a mess of it for me to bring you this morning." Thomas scowled and narrowed one eye in Harley's direction waiting for him to make some sort of defense. When the little man didn't say anything, Thomas jerked open the truck door and reached inside. It crossed Harley's mind his friend might have something in there to hit him with—one never knew what Thomas might do. He was not as unpredictable as back when he was drinking, but still...it gave Harley pause. When Thomas pulled out the food package and headed for the trailer, he growled, "Let's have some coffee."

Harley knew he couldn't avoid such a courtesy without arousing suspicion. The two had known one another since they were young. He pretty much knew what he could get away with...and what he couldn't. On the porch he reached to open the door and raised his voice several decibels and at least two octaves. "Come on in. The pot's still warm on the stove and there's plenty of it." He knew the breakfast dishes were already soaking in soapy water and out of sight. He couldn't recall anything that might give Eileen away. He could probably bull his way through this with a little luck.

Thomas shouldered his way past and sniffed. "Bacon, huh? You must not be as bad off as Lucy thinks you are."

Harley took the food from him without comment and deposited it in the refrigerator. "I picked up a few groceries yesterday but you tell Lucy this will be a welcome change from my own cooking. Last night I had some of that stew she brought over. You be sure and thank her for that, too."

Thomas sat down at the table watching as Harley poured two cups of coffee, brought them over, and sat one in front of him and the other just across the table. As he sipped from his cup, Thomas looked things over, noting the freshly painted baseboards, and seemed to relax a little.

"This is starting to look real nice, Harley. What's that door to the bedroom doing closed? It's going to get hot in here today; you ought to have that front window open…pull a little breeze through here." Thomas turned a little toward the door and moved as though to get up. "You want me to open that up? This wool shirt is getting warm."

Harley put a hand on his arm. "We can't open it."

"Why not?" Thomas had that suspicious little twist back in his voice like he might, all of a sudden, jump to a conclusion of some sort.

Harley didn't even have to think. "There's a rat in there…you know…a packrat. Must have gotten in through that front heater vent last night."

Thomas perked up at this. "Damn, Harley! You just had a rat in there a week ago. Don't you think you ought to do something about it?" Thomas looked around as though searching for something he could use as a cudgel. "Do you want me to help you corner the little bastard?" Thomas was always up for a little excitement. Anything, he would say, to lighten the day.

"No, no. I threw a bar-bait in there; once he settles down, he'll go ta eating it. It won't be long then till he's done for. I'm going to nail some tin over that hole under the vent. I think that's where they're getting in." Harley squinted hard at the door and pretended to listen for rat noises before going on. "Do you want a doughnut with that coffee? I just picked some up fresh yesterday at the store. Chocolate, too."

"Well, I don't mind if I do. I ate pretty early so I could get the kids off to school. Lucy was helping the old man with the sheep; he's taking them out today so she can work on a blanket." He smiled benignly. "I can hang out here and help you with the painting and then later we can go into town. They've got a new shipment of boots in at the Co-op; I was just thinking the other day we could both use a new pair."

"Oh, there's no need in you bothering to stick around. I know you're busy, what with the kids being home and all. And I've about finished with the paint work now." Harley thought from the beginning there might be some ulterior motive for Thomas's visit, and when he brought him the doughnut, he asked him straight up. "Is there something you want to talk about? You look a little down in the mouth to me. You and Lucy have a fight?"

"Naa, we don't fight much since I quit drinking." Thomas looked down at the doughnut but only pushed it around the saucer. "Charlie Yazzie brought some news yesterday evening." He paused and looked up at Harley, "I guess my dad is dead."

Harley wasn't expecting this and was somewhat taken aback. "Gilbert's dead! I didn't even know he was back in town."

"I didn't neither, really. I'd heard rumors, but I never really thought he'd be back...but he was. Now he's dead."

"Well, I'm sorry to hear that, buddy. I know you haven't seen him in a long time and didn't get along there for a lot a years...but still...it must be tough."

Thomas rubbed the back of his neck. "It didn't bother me so much there at first but when I woke up this morning it just sort of climbed all over me. I was just lying there in bed when it hit me, and for a minute, thought I was going to lose it. But you're right about one thing: there wasn't really much between us anymore, that's for sure. Still, I can't seem to get him out of my mind this morning. I told myself, 'He's just another dead drunk,' and then I realized I had been heading that same direction myself...before I quit drinking. If it hadn't been for the kids, I probably wouldn't have quit even then. At least that's what Lucy thinks. Maybe that's why my old man came back—maybe he thought this was the only thing he had to leave me."

Harley didn't know quite what to say to this. Thomas Begay had always been a private person and one who seldom showed any personal emotion.

Thomas could see Harley felt genuinely sorry about his father and that was enough to make him look away for a minute; when he turned back he smiled and winked. "If you don't need any help this morning I guess I just better get back and check on old Paul T'Sosi. He's only taking those sheep across the road today but that's where he damn near got run over that time before." The tall *Diné* rose from his chair, picked up his doughnut, and moved toward the

81

door. "I'll just take this along with me, if you don't mind. You sure you don't want help with that rat?"

Harley followed him out the door. "No, that's all right. It's probably already done for." Harley watched as Thomas Begay turned his truck around and headed for the highway; he paused before going back in the house. *That's a helluva thing about his father,* he thought. Though still feeling sorry for his friend, Harley was pretty sure Thomas meant this to be a lesson for him, as well. *Maybe that was the real reason he came out this morning.* No one ever thinks they will become a 'lost one' until it happens, and then, of course, it's usually too late to do anything about it.

When Harley Ponyboy went back into the trailer he knocked on the bedroom door and called softly to say Thomas was gone. Then he went back to the table to finish his coffee and doughnut.

Eileen first peeked out to make certain, then went directly to the window to look off down the road and assure herself the danger was past. "Why didn't you tell me there had been a rat in that bedroom last week?"

Harley didn't look up, took another bite of his doughnut, and then, after washing it down with a swallow of coffee, said, "First of all, Eileen, these aren't the same kind of rats they have in the city. These are packrats: little wild creatures that have been around as long as we have. They live on grass and seeds and such. They are quite clean, and in fact, our people have been eating them for maybe a thousand years—same as eating a rabbit really. We ate plenty of them when I was a kid up in Monument Valley. The old people liked them. They said, 'they are tender for our teeth and have a good flavor.' They're easy to come by, too. That can be important should times get hard and there's not much else to eat. They don't usually bother anyone. I just don't want them in the house—they chew the insulation off the electric wires. That wasn't so important before we got electricity, but now it could be a problem." He threw her a reassuring look. "Anyhow, Eileen, I already put a piece of tin over that hole after I trapped that first one. You won't be bothered with them."

Eileen opened the front door about half way and leaned against the frame as she breathed in what was left of the cool morning air. "It's going to get hot in here today."

R. Allen Chappell

8

Fallout

Charlie Yazzie found Monday mornings depressing. Legal Service's share of all the illicit, immoral, or criminal happenings of the weekend were generally dumped on his desk within an hour of coming in. Granted, he had the biggest desk in the office, but this morning, when he spread out the reports, there wasn't room enough left to set down a cup of coffee.

It was sometime past noon when Thomas Begay showed up, and when the receptionist told him to go on back to the office, he knew Charlie had been expecting him. The door was part way open so he didn't bother to knock; just went in and closed the door behind him. He sat in his usual chair and waited for the investigator to look up from his papers and when he did, Thomas gave a lift of his chin in greeting.

Charlie nodded and studied him a moment. "You okay this morning?"

Thomas nodded. "I'm good. I just got back from Harley's. Lucy sent me up there with some food. She always thinks he'll starve left on his own."

Charlie shook his head and smiled. "So how was Harley Ponyboy this morning?"

"Oh, he was fine. Best I've seen him for a while, actually." Thomas fiddled with his truck keys and wasn't really looking at Charlie when he said, "He's got some woman living with him...a full-time night woman, unless I miss my guess."

"Really! Who is she?" Charlie was genuinely surprised.

"I have no idea who she is. Harley was hiding her in the front bedroom. It's no wonder he can't win a hand at poker." Thomas chuckled to himself, "I can read that boy like a book."

"You never saw the woman? Don't know what she looks like?"

"Nope. I knew when I first drove up in the yard but didn't say anything. I figured he'd mention something when he was ready, but he never did. Unless, of course, he's taken to wearing ladies' underwear."

"Please tell me you didn't see him wearing ladies' underwear."

"No, but there were two pair hanging on that old clothes line of Anita's. I'll bet she would be mad as hell at that." He looked up at Charlie from under the brim of his hat and smiled. "If a little gust of wind hadn't come up just as I pulled in I wouldn't have seen them at all, but just for a second, there they were, flapping in the breeze."

"Well, I'll be go to hell." Charlie grinned, "And he never said a word about her the whole time you were there?"

"No...no he didn't, and that's what pisses me off. Gave me some phony story about having a rat

85

trapped in the bedroom—said he'd taken care of it already." Now both men were chuckling. Thomas slapped his leg. "He's apparently doing all right though. They had bacon for breakfast and there was a fresh box of doughnuts open. Maybe he's found himself a rich woman? And here Lucy thought he was living on potted meat and crackers out there."

"Why do you suppose he didn't say anything about her?" Charlie could come up with several reasons right off the top of his head.

Thomas was thinking the same way. "You figure maybe he's ashamed of her...or her, of him?"

"Maybe it's someone's wife or girlfriend?"

Neither man thought this last thought much of a possibility. They couldn't see Harley making so bold as to lure away someone else's woman; and she would have to be a desperate woman at that.

"Whatever the case, I don't think we should tell the girls. I know it would be hard for Sue to keep a secret like that, and this is obviously something Harley doesn't want known. I believe we'd best just keep this to ourselves for now."

Thomas smiled and agreed it was Harley's business, however outrageous the details might turn out to be.

Charlie shook his head to clear any remaining thoughts of what Thomas would later refer to as 'Harley's affair', then picked up a folder. "Billy Red Clay's not happy with us this morning."

"He knows about us being down at the Social Club?"

"I finally had to tell him but I think we can trust him to keep it quiet, if at all possible." Charlie held up a report. "I did receive this about an hour ago. Billy's apparently not so upset as to take me out of the loop. It's the investigative report on old man Klee's pickup. It's about what we thought: whoever killed the old man knew what he was doing. The Feds went over the truck with a fine-tooth comb, according to Billy, and came up with almost nothing. They're running what few prints they lifted—old prints for the most part, they think—probably from Benny's family or whatever. I expect it'll take a while to sort those out. The only other thing they found was a blue silk...uh, I guess you would call it a bookmark for lack of a better word; at least that's how Billy described it. It had some gold lettering that read, Living Clean and that's all it said."

Thomas was listening but finding it hard to concentrate. Thoughts of his father wandered through his head—scenes from his childhood mainly—those being the only happy times he remembered with his father. He finally stood and walked over to the window to avoid embarrassing himself. After a minute or so he wandered back to his chair but still didn't trust his voice. He just let Charlie continue talking about the old silversmith's murder.

The Investigator pretended not to notice and appeared to be absorbed in the report. "Billy added a little note here at the end," he said, finally, tapping the page. "He mentions the FBI can find not a single witness who saw the person who parked that truck in the lot behind the Social Club." He went on, "This, though it had to have been dropped off in the early morning hours, essentially broad daylight. The Feds seem willing to believe the driver simply got lucky and walked away." Charlie looked up. "But you and I both know those Indians that hang out down there wouldn't talk to a Federal Agent, let alone admit to seeing anything."

"You're not saying we should go back to Rosie's again?"

"No, that's pretty much off the table at this point. What I am saying is someone, somewhere, knows who brought that truck into town. There's something here I'm missing and I intend to find out what."

Thomas, who was a great believer in luck, was not so sure. "Well, you let me know if you come up with something...pretty much looks like a dead-end to me."

Charlie nodded but was not yet ready to say what was in the back of his mind. One thing was for certain; he had already put Thomas on the spot once and he wasn't willing to go that route again.

~~~~~~

Sue Hanagarni-Yazzie listened, with the receiver tight against her ear, blocking out her young son who was in a temper. This was the second time Lucy Tallwoman had called. The first time, Sue had been outside in her garden to pick a few tomatoes for supper, and did not reach the phone in time to answer. Since Lucy's new phone was installed, the pair usually spent a few minutes each day talking about one small thing or another. She was sure her friend would call back.

When Sue again motioned young Joseph Wiley to come in from his place—half-in and half-out of the screen door—the boy's attitude turned even more surly. He frowned and shook his head. "No! I want outside...I wanta' feed the horses." The boy fell to muttering under his breath making his obstinate face as he glared at his mother. Exasperated, Sue gave him an equally determined look, and warned, "How would you like a big fat spanking this morning. I may even tell your father how you are and he will give you another spanking when he gets home." She threatened all this though the boy seldom received as much as a swat on the behind and by now had grown impervious to such exaggerated threats.

"I'm going to call him at work right now," Sue bluffed, picking up the phone. "He'll be angry. He doesn't like to be called at his office just to deal with bad little boys." The two stared at one another for nearly a full minute before the boy lowered his gaze and came inside—purposely slamming the screen door behind him. He watched to see if his mother would acknowledge this door slamming to be the final word in the incident. He knew not to push Sue too far, however, and took notice when she shook a finger in his direction. "If you slam that door again and wake the baby, you'll be sorry."

Sue was a progressive Navajo mother who read books on child rearing and was not always sure the old Navajo way, of letting a child do as they pleased was the right approach. When she was a child, a traditional *Diné* mother saw no harm in a child acting up, occasionally, as long as no real harm came of it. And *that* mother might not have the final word in the matter anyway; her brother, if she had one, could take charge if he saw fit. It was an uncle's place to over-see certain aspects of a nephew's upbringing. The same was true for a girl; she often depended on an aunt or even older cousin for guidance. In so matri-lineal a society a child's father, traditionally, had surprisingly little say in such matters.

In olden times, a certain amount of independence was thought to build character in a child. It was thought they learned from their own mistakes that way and were then encouraged to be self-reliant—the better to prepare themselves for a life in those far more difficult times.

Sue found she was not alone in her more modern approach to child rearing. She had no brother or sister herself, and despite what Charlie's Aunt Annie thought, she and her husband intended to raise their children as they saw fit. Charlie took an equal role in the boy's upbringing despite traditional attitudes to the contrary.

This current standoff between mother and son was interrupted by Lucy Tallwoman's second call. She had guessed her friend was probably occupied with the baby or temporarily, out of hearing. Lucy felt it rude to let a phone ring on and on, but decided now to give it another go, and this time let it ring just a bit longer.

Sue picked up the phone on its fourth ring and Lucy Tallwoman's relaxed and almost imperturbable aura, even over the phone, seemed to promote a calming effect. Maybe Lucy would have some ideas in regard to her stubborn son. Though her friend was more traditional than she, Sue had noticed, of late, the new influx of money from Lucy's weaving seemed to be having an impact—leaving her open to more progressive thinking. *Slowly, the Begays are coming into the modern world,* she thought. She and Charlie might be partially responsible for this and she hoped it would prove to be a good influence. That was not always the case when traditional minded people changed too quickly. Sue had seen it before.

~~~~~~~

When Charlie came up the drive that evening the first thing he saw was Thomas Begay coming down the lane on the resurrected tractor. Joseph Wiley, grinning ear to ear, was sitting on his lap. Charlie smiled at the pair as he pulled abreast of them.

"Two fouled injectors!" Thomas called above the clatter of the little diesel engine. "That's all it was! I was able to clean them myself and didn't have to buy any new ones."

Joseph Wiley waved excitedly at his father and called, "It's fixed now…Thomas has fixed it!" Charlie nodded to them both and pulled on up to the house. Sue was standing on the front porch holding the baby who reached out her chubby little arms to him. She was going to be a daddy's girl; that's what everyone said. As she passed the toddler over to her husband, Sue gave Charlie a worried look. "I was talking to Lucy earlier; she hasn't seen Harley Ponyboy lately. Lucy said Thomas went out to his place and Harley seemed all right to him. He said he had just been busy on his trailer."

Charlie smiled to himself. "Oh, I wouldn't worry about Harley Ponyboy. When he hears this tractor is fixed he'll be by to borrow it in no time, I'll bet. Harley mentioned to us at the auction he had some work to do on that sand-wash behind his place." Charlie did his best to keep a straight face as he carried his daughter down the driveway to watch her brother 'drive' the tractor.

"We should build a shed for this tractor. It shouldn't sit out in the weather—especially this winter." Thomas liked to think ahead when it came to machinery but was not all that particular in thinking ahead when it came to most other things.

Charlie frowned, "I expect a shed will have to wait until I can make up what the tractor cost. You didn't tell me it would need a shed."

"It doesn't *have* to have one but it will save you money over the long haul...maintenance and all." Thomas handed over Charlie's son and now the investigator had a child in each arm. "I was in town this afternoon to make arrangements for my father and pick up what he had on him when he died—not that it was much. Funny thing is...was they didn't find any money on him. I'd just given him a few dollars and he never even made it to the other bar, apparently. I just can't figure out what's become of it, that's all."

"Did they say if the death certificate had been issued yet?" Charlie was curious.

"Not yet. The coroner said the lab results from the autopsy are on hold for some reason; he thinks they could be in tomorrow. The county cops learned, from one of the people where Gilbert was staying, that he was seen talking with a man a short time before his death. But the undersheriff didn't attach any real importance to it. Their office had pretty much concluded it was natural causes from the start. They don't seem to feel any further investigation is needed." Thomas paused as he recalled what the undersheriff mentioned. "He said my old man had been doing some odd jobs around town and had been able to pay for his room, at least. About the only thing he had on him, though, was an old wallet with his PRCA association card...and a few pictures." Thomas reached in his pocket, "...and this," he said, holding out a blue silk bookmarker with the words 'Living Clean' printed on it. "This was in his pocket along with some change."

Charlie stared at the bookmarker before raising his eyes back to Thomas. "This is just like the one found in Benny's old truck."

Thomas nodded, "I mentioned that to the undersheriff, and he thought someone might have been passing them out around town—some religious organization maybe."

Charlie nodded. "Maybe." But he was frowning when he said it and Thomas took this to mean he wasn't convinced.

After Thomas Begay parked the tractor and said his goodbyes, he fired up his truck and left for home, without further ado. Charlie stood staring after him thinking about Gilbert Nez. He then put his son down, hefted the baby to his shoulders, and went to feed the horses. Joseph Wiley had to trot to keep up—all the while keeping a wary eye out for the formidable band of guineas roaming the neighborhood. The boy's pup followed so closely he almost became entangled with the child's feet. He, too, however, kept a cautious eye out for the nefarious fowl.

9

The Vixen

Harley Ponyboy sat in a metal lawn chair on his rickety back porch. He'd built it soon after finishing the front porch—both now going to hell, as he put it. He fingered the chair's worn paint and wondered if it had ever even seen a lawn; not in the ten years since he bought it at the yard sale in Kirtland that was for certain.

Due to recent rains the wash behind the trailer was running water—quite a lot of water for the time of year. It was slowly eating away at the shallow bank and was now no more than fifty feet from the back door. There was a time when Harley wouldn't have cared if the whole place was swept away. The coming of Eileen Smith had changed everything bringing a better sort of life within his grasp. He was determined to make the best of so rare an opportunity.

"So, what do you think?" Eileen asked, coming out on the back porch, turning around, and throwing the towel off her dripping hair. She had cut it fashionably short and dyed it black. She whirled—flinging little beads of light in the afternoon sun.

Harley, though taken by surprise at the new look, was aware that saying just the right thing could be critically important at this point. He studied her carefully, for an embarrassingly long moment, before answering in an unsure voice. "It makes you look…more Indian, I guess. Younger, too—I like it." This was apparently the right thing to say. And he beamed as she broke into a smile.

"Good. I was hoping that would be your impression. I've always felt reinventing one's self, from time to time, never hurts a person."

"Well, it looks very nice on you."

"Thank you and it's very good of you to say so, too." Eileen was beginning to suspect she had fallen into a situation with distinct possibilities despite what little she might have to work with.

Harley, again, felt caught up in that indefinable glow of well-being that had for so long eluded him and was reaffirmed in his newfound belief there might be better times to come. Eileen perched herself on a porch railing and the two of them sat quietly, looking across at one another, each with their own quite different thoughts.

Both heard the sound of the engine at the same time and then the tortured squeal of a truck's brakes coming down the little incline before the slight climb to the trailer. Eileen came instantly alert. "Sounds like you have company." She jumped to her feet and headed for the back door."

Harley frowned. "Don't worry yourself, Eileen. I'll take care of it." He came around the back of the trailer to see Alfred Nakii sitting in his truck, watching the front door, about to sound his horn: that being the proper thing to do on the *Dinétah*. Only very close friends or relatives would think of getting out and knocking at the door.

"Yaa' eh t'eeh," Alfred called out as he saw Harley coming around the end of the trailer. He gestured with his chin. "I saw your truck and figured you were at home." He got down and the men shook hands as Harley returned the greeting.

Cocking his head to one side, Harley inquired how things were going for his neighbor.

"Oh, everything is fine, Harley. I just come from Farmington and thought you might like to know…there's talk down at Rosie's place…some stranger is looking for a small red-haired woman—about like the one I dropped off here a few days ago, I guess." Alfred looked away when he added, "No one knows what he wants with her. It could be anything, I guess." And here his neighbor was quick to reassure, "…but I never said nothing about her to no one." He gestured toward the trailer with a push of his lips. "If she's still here you might want to see if she knows who that man could be," he shrugged. "He could be her husband, or even the law, though they say he don't look like a law. Anyways, I thought you might like to hear it. You never know these days what people are up to."

Harley listened without any discernible change in his expression, and waited until Alfred was completely through before nodding. "I appreciate that, Alfred, but that woman is gone now; she left the next day. She said she was headed ta Albuquerque. I doubt we'll be seeing her again...if she was the woman they were talking about."

Alfred nodded his head and was satisfied he had done the right thing back there in town. Harley had always been good to him, and to his mother, too, back when she was alive. A Navajo of the old sort doesn't forget that sort of thing.

Harley knew Alfred didn't believe Eileen was gone, of course, and didn't expect him to. But he knew Alfred would not tell anyone about her being there now. It's just the way people used to be before things changed on the reservation. The two men talked a while longer: Alfred assuring his friend he was there should help of any kind be needed.

"Well, I've been thinking I'd take a little trip up ta visit relatives. If you see me gone I'd appreciate it if you could feed Jake for me from time ta time. If you see you can't, just turn him loose. He'll stick around and be all right—if he don't get himself run over.

"Oh, I'd be happy to see to him for you. There won't be any need to turn him loose."

As his neighbor got back in his truck he turned and looked at Harley a final time. "Oh, I almost forgot. That man is staying in one of Rosie's upstairs rooms at the Social Club and he's saying around that he will give a reward to anyone who knows where to find that woman...just so you know." He put the truck in gear and winked at Harley Ponyboy as he backed out of the yard.

Harley stood looking toward the corral and Jake, who in turn watched him, making sure it wasn't time to eat. Mules have an inner time clock that alerts them within a few minutes of their regular feeding hour. It wasn't time yet and Jake knew it, still...if Harley was drunk things could change. Jake was a mule that liked to cover his bases.

With a final calculating glance at the mule, the little man went back in the trailer and sat down at the table. Eileen came from the bedroom, moved directly to the stove, and put coffee on. Neither of them spoke, just waited for the coffee to perk, and when it was done she brought two steaming cups and sat across from him. "So, what did Alfred want?"

Harley took his time doctoring his coffee to suit him, and then, without looking up, and in a low voice, said, "Alfred says there is a man in town looking for you—he's offering money ta anyone who might have information." He took a cautious sip of the hot liquid before looking up to see a flicker of what he thought could be fear cross her face. Still she didn't speak as her face became an inscrutable mask.

"Why is this man looking for you, Eileen?" Harley did his best to remain calm as though just making conversation. He'd already thought of everything it could be, but still was not ready for the answer when it came.

"He wants to kill me," and she didn't bother to look away when she said it. "His name is Claude Bell. He came to the Rehabilitation Center in Phoenix just after I did. He's part Indian...that's what he said... and he seemed nice at first. Told me we Indians had to stick together. He was on parole but admitted he'd started drinking again after they let him out and said he thought it might be getting the best of him. His parole officer got him into the program at the Bible center. He and I became friends—you know how it is with drunks—they tend to hook up with other drunks."

Harley nodded—being well aware of the truth in this.

She toyed nervously with her cup and pointed to the stove to see if Harley wanted more coffee.

He put a hand over his cup indicating he didn't and found himself fighting back a wave of sympathy for the woman.

"But why would this guy want to kill you Eileen?"

"I know things, Harley—I got lucky and was able to get away—but I knew he'd come after me. He's smart...and he's killed before...maybe more than once." Eileen's features were an emotional desert betrayed only by an almost indiscernible hint of dread. "He and I were members of the same Bible sales team—canvassing the poorer neighborhoods and contacting local businesses for donations. Selling Bibles is how the outreach center supports itself...along with a few government grants and individual contributions. Our team leader was a recovering alcoholic himself. He lived at the center and was the director's right-hand man. He had, several times, cautioned everyone not to let personal relationships get in the way of our goals. "Sobriety First," he told us. He also made it clear that alcoholics, in early recovery, seldom make reliable support people." She forced a laugh. "Boy, was he right about that."

Harley nodded and tried not to show his concern for where this was going.

"One night, Claude smuggled in a bottle and we hid out in the laundry room. Like a fool I let him convince me we could get away with it...you know...that a couple of drinks wouldn't hurt." Eileen shook her head. "My father always said I was a stupid girl, and I guess I was out to prove him right. Apparently, someone from our team spotted us and reported back to the leader. When he found us, there was a terrible row and he told me to go to my room." Eileen gasped softly, as though she'd remembered something and suddenly couldn't get enough air; she paused to gather herself.

Harley squirmed in his chair suddenly not sure he wanted to hear what was coming, and all the while knowing there was no choice. The genie was out of the bottle and he was afraid now where that might lead. He gestured for Eileen to continue in spite of himself.

She took a sip of coffee and a large gulp of air as she attempted to collect herself. Harley knew she was putting the thing together in her mind—as much for herself as for him. Through the window he saw clouds building a dark line to the west and thought he could smell rain through the open door.

Eileen, staring through that same window, was unable for a moment to tear her eyes away; then she eventually turned back to Harley to continue her tale.

"The next morning, I came awake to the sound of people running up and down the halls. The place was already a mess—cops everywhere—and several people rounded up for questioning, but there was no Claude Bell to be found. He'd slipped away hours before the body was discovered." She hesitated, her voice only a whisper. "Our team leader was dead—throat slashed with a box cutter—they found him lying in a pool of blood. Claude used a box cutter in the shipping room from time to time and carried it with him everywhere." Eileen feared for a moment she wouldn't be able to continue, but choking back a sob, forced herself to go on. She knew Harley needed to hear it; though at times he appeared on the verge of stopping her himself. She only shook her head—held up a hand for quiet—and went on.

"I saw right away I was in serious trouble. Not from the police necessarily, but from Claude. He knew I was the only real witness...and that he'd previously said things he wouldn't have if he had been sober. I managed to get out through the kitchen area, and with only the clothes on my back, headed down the alleyway for my old car. I kept it up the block at the house of an old lady who's a friend of mine. I sold her a Bible once, and from time to time, stopped by to see if she needed anything. She was a good person; one of the few friends I had there."

"They let you have a car?"

"We weren't supposed to have a car, of course, but several people did; they just couldn't keep them on campus." Eileen sucked in a long ragged breath and continued, "When I jumped in, and started the engine, Claude raised up a little from the back and gave me a sign to stay calm. He said he would get us out of the situation and no one would get hurt." Eileen grimaced. "I knew someone had already gotten hurt and he probably wouldn't hesitate to do the same to me, should I not play along." Eileen's hands were shaking now and her lower lip quivered.

"I only had two months left at the center. And I'd agreed to live with my Aunt Mary outside Salt

Lake—at least until I got on my feet. My mother wanted no part of me. She made a point of letting me know she'd sent a letter to my father—wherever *he* was—and my uncle, asking if either of them might have a place for me. She told me she never heard back from them.

"It was my Aunt Mary that finally stepped up; she said she had a job lined up for me in that little town in Utah where she lived. She even co-signed for my car loan so I'd have a way home and be able to get back and forth to work when I got there. But later I think she, too, started having second thoughts. She was married with a husband and two young children of her own."

Eileen paused, seemed to ponder a moment, before heaving a sigh of remorse. "As long as I've gone this far I may as well tell you the rest. Claude was in prison for armed robbery before being paroled, and later was referred to the Bible center. He and two friends were involved in the armed robbery of a liquor store. The store's owner was shot, and though badly wounded, still managed to reach his own gun and return fire. One of Claude's partners was hit and died instantly. When Claude was finally caught, he claimed he and his remaining friend were only customers in the store and had no part in the crime. The prosecutor didn't buy it, of course, and slapped them with murder in the first degree." Eileen thought back, determined to get the next part of the story exactly right.

"On the night we were drinking, Claude told me it was him that actually did the shooting—trying to impress me with how macho he was, I guess. He told me *he* killed the liquor store owner, but of course, at first, he tried to convince authorities it had been the third guy...the now dead friend...who'd done the shooting. The prosecutor didn't believe the story, but was left with little evidence to the contrary. Finally, he agreed to cut them a deal rather than see them walk. The plea bargain still involved a lot of years behind bars but they figured it was better than a murder one charge. So, they took the deal." Here, Eileen stopped to gauge how Harley was taking her story. Seeing only sympathetic encouragement, she went on. "Maricopa County takes murder in the commission of an armed robbery very seriously, Harley."

Harley was not without experience in the legal system, though certainly not on a scale such as this. He nodded, silently acknowledging the gravity of the charges.

"Claude Bell did eventually get out," Eileen went on, "but his partner was killed in prison. The cops suspected, at the time, Claude was involved in that death, too, but again they had nothing they felt would hold up in court, and they had to let him out when his time was finally up. Claude probably thought his partner would eventually turn state's evidence and maybe finger him as the shooter in the holdup, if only to lighten his own load." Eileen's shoulders slumped as she took a sip of her now cold coffee. "I must be an idiot to get mixed up with that guy. Now I guess I pay the price...one way or the other."

"How did you get away from him, Eileen?"

"It wasn't easy. We wouldn't have made it as far as we did if I hadn't saved a little money back from what my Aunt had been sending me occasionally. She had a good job and so did her husband and she said they could afford it."

"So...what happened then?"

"So...we pulled into a gas station at Tuba city. After Claude filled the tank, he said he had to use the restroom—I had already gone while he was gassing up. As soon as he paid the cashier, and I saw him head for the restrooms, that's when I just took off. I ran the hell out of that car until just before Tonalea; that's when the engine cratered. I was lucky there was a kid on his way into town who stopped. He said he lived just up the road and told me his father fixed cars. He said if his dad couldn't fix it for me he might still buy it...and he did. That gave me fifty bucks...but no car. The son gave me a ride into Kayenta and I hitched from there. I knew Claude would be right behind me but it's not as easy for a man to get rides as it is for a woman. I hoped to stay ahead of him until I could lose myself somewhere on the reservation. So here I am. I guess you got lucky, huh, Harley?"

Harley unconsciously made a little sound of sympathy as he looked down at the table. "Well, it's not hard, now, to see why you would be trying to lay low, Eileen." He looked up then, as though something else occurred to him. "What were *you* in the half-way house for, Eileen?"

"Me? Oh, I was just a drunk. I finally sunk so low I signed myself into the Bible Center's program—on the recommendation of my social worker. I had to sign a contract and everything." She made a grim face. "I guess turning a drunk around is a tougher business than I thought."

"I know what you're talking about, Eileen. I have been bad ta drink for a long time myself...sober over a year now...but that don't mean much with me. My friend Thomas says he and I will always be just one drink away from bein' drunks again." Harley bit his lower lip. "I know he's right, too. I've quit a bunch of times—never for as long as Thomas—but he has a wife and kids ta look after." Harley smiled over at her. "At least that's the excuse I use when I take off on a bender." Harley wanted her to understand that he, too, had his demons.

"So, what's the verdict, Harley? Am I down the road or what?" There was a catch in Eileen's voice and the last vestige of bravado slipped away as she lifted her head to look him in the eye. This Harley Ponyboy was now the only person she had to turn to; and when he seemed at a loss for words, she murmured, "I'll get my stuff together...and that won't take long."

Harley shook his head, held up a hand, and with a half-smile assured Eileen, "This don't change anything for me, Ms...Smith...is it?"

Eileen managed a weak smile. "Oh...that. I was pretty sure you knew it wasn't Smith—but it is still Eileen—Eileen May, actually. I know my Navajo name, too. My Aunt Mary told me its *Atsii At'ee*. But I guess we better stick with Smith for now."

Harley rolled the Navajo words around on his tongue and smiled, "Antelope Girl, huh? I think that is a fine name."

The two sat across from one another, each trying to get their head around where they were going and where that might leave them. Neither had a clue what they were in for.

10

Home

Well after midnight, Harley's old truck was still some miles from their turnoff. Eileen sat slumped against the passenger side door sound asleep. and Harley looked over at her from time to time trying to keep from dozing off himself. He thought he should warn her again about the door, but hated to wake her. He had taken the precaution of jamming a screwdriver between the door and the frame hoping that would help.

It was a gray fox, jumping out in front of them, that finally cured his drowsiness. He hit the brakes and swerved—nearly throwing Eileen through the windshield—which was fortunate as the door he had fixed popped open, and she was lucky not to fall out. She caught herself and glanced over at Harley, saying. "What the hell…?" She straightened, pulled the door shut, and leaned forward a bit to peer out the windshield.

"You're not falling asleep are you, Harley?"

"Not now, I'm not." He looked over and grinned. Harley had always maintained that a person was better off running over a small animal than risk going off the road and maybe getting someone killed. He was also aware few people seem able to make that reflexive decision in time to avoid a catastrophe.

"You said you fixed that Goddamned door!"

"No, as I recall, I said I thought it was fixed— but that you should be careful of it."

Eileen glared across at him but was too tired to argue. "How much longer is this going to take?" She frowned. "Will there be some daylight by the time we reach the turnoff?" She peered out the side window into the velvety darkness, shaking her head to clear the cobwebs, and fighting back doubts that continued to plague her every waking moment. Despite Harley's assurances, she couldn't help wondering if this truly was her only option. She couldn't imagine taking off into the backcountry in the dark. Harley already told her it was rough going up there— dangerous even—for someone who didn't know the country. "Some of these roads aren't even on the map. That's what makes it the right place for us," he assured her.

Far up a canyon, south and west of Monument Valley, Harley Ponyboy had family ties, clansmen mostly; he seriously doubted anyone could find them once they were off the main roads. Dawn finally began sketching the nearest buttes in silver, and the hoodoos were brought to a ghostly reality. He was just pointing out some of the more interesting rock formations when the turnoff appeared. Harley gently tapped the brakes and eased onto a side road.

After an additional bone-jarring hour, Eileen saw what he meant by isolated. *Why would anyone want to live out here?* They passed several abandoned hogans, one with a large hole knocked in the side, probably, she thought, *to allow the escape of some dead person's chindi spirit.* Her mother told her all about those evil spirits and the damage they could do, should they take a notion, but it had made little impression at the time.

They passed yet another dwelling. An old couple stood in the first rays of the morning sun to watch as a young boy and his dog pushed a flock of mongrel sheep to a distant line of hills. Eileen slowly shook her head as she watched the boy. *No more than nine or ten years old, what sort of future does that boy have to look forward to?*

"Now, who did you say I would be staying with?" She couldn't remember him mentioning a name.

"My mother's sister—not her real sister you understand—she's her clan sister...a cousin of hers, I think."

"She lives all alone out here?" Just the thought of it gave Eileen a chill.

Harley turned slightly while keeping one eye on the road. "Auntie Willie is not exactly alone. But she did set her husband's saddle outside the hogan years ago... so only she and her father live there now."

"She sat his saddle outside the door? What's that supposed to mean?"

Harley smiled as he thought about how to put it. "I was only a boy at the time, myself, but I remember asking my grandmother the same thing. 'How can it be that a woman has only to set her man's saddle outside the door and she is then divorced—just like that? The man never even tries to come back?' "

"My grandmother said, 'That is just the way it has always been with our people.' So...a woman who finds she can't get along with her husband and decides she wants him to go away will do that thing with his saddle. Then he has no choice but to go and leave her alone. If he didn't, he would not be at one with his people and he'd even risk reprisal from his wife's family." Harley chuckled at the matter-of-fact simplicity of the thing. It showed the wisdom of his people, he thought. "Eileen, you'll like these folks we are going to see. They are old school Navajo. You might learn a lot about your *Diné* side from them and probably a lot about your white self, too; in fact, I'd almost bet on it."

"So they don't have running water, right?"

"Well, of course they do, Eileen. They are at the upper end of the canyon. Yellow Rock Spring runs right past the hogan. Good water, and plenty of it, at least this time of year. Later on, maybe not so much, but you will be gone before then."

Eileen felt a shiver run through her—she was a town girl and knew this was not going to be easy, but thought at the time *it will be easier than what's waiting for me back in town.* Claude Bell finding her was something she didn't even want to consider.

In the first flush of sunrise, the rust-stained walls of the canyon took on a crimson glow and a breeze wafted, clear and cool, down the big wash. At midday, a slack tide in the diurnal flow would bring a delicious stillness along with an almost palpable, soul-soothing quiet. The respite would last only an hour or two. Then the return flow of warm air would start back up the canyon, sometimes building to a strong breeze, which would then blow until dusk. Harley Ponyboy drank it all in and was happy in that way people sometimes are when revisiting a place of fond memories.

The harder the climb, and the rougher the climb, the more Eileen's doubts grew. By the time they finally jolted and jounced their way up yet another side canyon, she was ready to throw in the towel.

When Harley finally stopped the truck in a little whirlwind of dust, she turned. "I can't do this!" she murmured."

"Can't do what, Eileen?" Harley turned to see the expression on her face; she cringed as she looked about the little clearing in the cedars. The hogan was a big one, but old, showing the many different colors of mud chinking that washed down the creek over the years. The main dwelling was flanked on one side by the ubiquitous brush arbor, or summer hogan. Eileen could make out rudimentary cooking facilities, and across from that, some chairs and a cot. There was a '50s Ford pickup parked off to one side and an ancient horse drawn wagon lay broken and splintered; a sad reminder of an era that now seemed to make no sense. Neither vehicle had moved in years; the truck's wheels buried deep in dried mud from the he-rains. The two visitors rolled down their respective windows and listened to the great soughing of the wind through the juniper and stunted pine. There was a rustling of oak brush above the clearing and, somewhere beyond that, the comforting sound of running water.

Eileen May took no solace from these things and drew further within herself. "I can't live out here,

Harley, I'd go crazy. What do these people do all day? There's nothing here." Her voice sank nearly to a whisper, "People don't really live like this...do they?"

Harley smiled. "You won't be living here, Eileen. You'll only be their guest for a few days, that's all. You won't have ta do anything you don't want to." He smiled. "It might be a good chance ta study your Bible. Remember how you said it would comfort a person during bad times?"

As they talked, a dog broke from the brush barking only once before rushing the truck. He then stood his ground, growling at Eileen, and daring her to step down. An older woman came from the creek with a bucket that slopped water as she walked, spilling some down her long skirt. A small woman, no taller than Eileen, bent now with age and certainly never as attractive.

The older woman paused to stare at so unlikely a thing as visitors, then recognizing Harley Ponyboy, her eyes lit up. She called off the dog and waved one arm toward the hogan as she continued in that direction—she did not set the bucket down nor did she slacken her pace.

Harley got down from the truck and went around to Eileen's side to remove the screwdriver jammed in the door. Eileen stepped out, but stayed close to the truck, suspiciously eyeing the dog that stood back now, but did not wag his tail or grin at them. "Will that thing bite me?" She got no immediate response and continued to hang back.

Harley smiled at his aunt and waved back. He then reached into the bed of the truck lifting out a large cardboard box of things they'd brought from his trailer. Eileen stood quietly for another moment; the dog causing her to form an even more hopeless opinion of the place. Now, on the ground, she couldn't help feeling vulnerable and reluctant to move away from the escape pod of Harley's truck.

"A-hah-la'nih," the woman called from the doorway, finally setting her bucket down, and coming toward them with a smile, which turned to a questioning glance as she looked Eileen over with that curiosity peculiar to those from isolated places with few people.

Harley returned the old woman's affectionate greeting, giving his aunt a warm hug, before turning back to his companion, who he politely introduced but without offering details as to who she might be or their relationship.

His Aunt Willie Etcitty nodded her head at him and said in Navajo, "You have not been here in a long time, Nephew." She paused to glance again at Eileen but just as quickly turned back to Harley. "Is this your new woman, then?" She clucked to herself and bit her lip to prevent saying something she might later regret. Finally, she whispered, "She's not so big as that other one you had before." And couldn't help adding, "I just hope she is a little better natured," and grinned to show she was only half-serious.

"No, Auntie, my wife died some time back. I'm sure someone must have told you that by now."

The woman paused, and squinted past them, giving every appearance she was indeed thinking about it. "Hmm... yes," she finally nodded. "I guess I did hear that. You are so seldom around this country now—I never know what's going on with you for sure." She looked away for a moment then murmured, "I am sorry to hear about your other wife Nephew...but if you'll recall, I never took much to that woman." She glanced thoughtfully at Eileen again. "I suppose things have a way of turning out for the best after all." She and Harley then spoke for a few minutes more in Navajo before turning back to Eileen who had been standing quietly looking from one to the other as they spoke. Harley could see she understood almost nothing of their conversation, and she appeared to him as though she might bolt for the truck at any second. He moved closer and laid a hand on her shoulder in reassurance, saying under his breath, "It will be fine, Eileen. I can see she likes you already. Her name is Willie but you know older people out here don't much use a person's real name, at least not in that person's presence. "

Eileen showed her teeth and asked in a grim whisper, "What do I call her then...Harley's Aunt?"

"No, just Auntie will be fine." She understands more English than she lets on, so don't let her act otherwise with you. You probably already know enough words to get along. Her father is at a sing over by Big Indian Mountain and won't be back for a few days. You'll have some time to get acquainted."

"Her father...my God, how old is *he*?"

Harley's aunt, suddenly willing to understand English, threw back her head. "He's eighty-six years old—too old to be running off all over the country going to sings." She chortled. "He says he's looking for a new wife," and shook her head again. "I don't know what the man would do with another wife if he

115

found one...my mother has been gone for thirty years." She raised her hands. "I ask him why he waited so long to start looking for a new woman. He said he had needed the rest."

This made Eileen smile and she began to think she could get along with this aunt of Harley's...for a few days anyway.

Willie, she went on to tell Eileen, was short for Willamina, which was her name on the Tribal Rolls. "That name was too hard for some people to say, so I'm just Willie, now. A person isn't remembered much for their name anyway; it's their *hozo* and how they treat other people that they become known for. But I guess a person has to have some kind of name, and Willie is mine." The woman smiled her way through this but it was plain to see her name had long been a sticking point, and something she wanted to clear up right off the bat.

While Eileen was putting away her things in the hogan, Harley fell back into Navajo with his aunt. He spoke quietly—telling her she shouldn't let anyone know Eileen was up there and to not even mention her to anyone.

"Why is that, Nephew? Are you ashamed of her? She seems presentable enough to me though she could do with some sturdier clothes for out here. That fancy dress won't last long in the brush. She knows about going to the bathroom outside, I hope?"

Harley sighed and admitted Willie might have to explain a few things to Eileen. He then told his aunt he had to go back into town—maybe for as long as a few days—on "unfinished business." He said he would be back for Eileen as soon as possible.

His aunt nodded agreeably to all this and said she would make his woman as comfortable as she could, but hoped she wouldn't expect too much of them. She thought her nephew was still the same boy he had always been; a boy with a good heart.

Now in a hurry, Harley took only a few minutes to say goodbye to Eileen, explaining he had to talk to Charlie Yazzie. Charlie would find a way to help her. He again assured her she was safe there and he would be back as soon as he could.

She knew Harley was trying to do the right thing by her, but privately, Eileen wondered if someone like Harley...or even his friend Charlie Yazzie...was up to dealing with her problem? Claude Bell was a streetwise and ruthless killer.

Willie Etcitty caught the expression on Eileen's face and knew instantly what she was thinking. She realized then just how little the woman knew about Harley Ponyboy, and how much she had left to learn.

He was almost back to the highway when Harley remembered he hadn't asked his Aunt Willie if she still had the 'Long Colt' given her by her grandfather. The revolver should rightfully have gone to a grandson, but he'd had none. The old man did not give it to his son, he said, for fear it might wind up in the 'old pawn' at the trader's.

That pistol, according to the grandfather, had once belonged to a white man who had come riding through *his* grandfather's summer camp on Montezuma Creek. It happened well south of Bluff, Utah, in 1902, during the Time of Ripening Corn.

The stranger was wearing only a pair of pants, his socks, and the pistol. He hadn't eaten in two days, he told the Navajo, and didn't even have a blanket except the one under his saddle, which he only had use of when it wasn't on the horse.

The Indians gave him something to eat and drink, and after that the man offered to trade for a fresh mount, and a blanket in return for his jaded horse and empty pistol. He had no cartridges for the gun, he admitted. The Indians thought this somewhat strange. *Why would someone carry an empty gun around with him?* The white man's horse was on its last legs and worn out, but obviously well-bred. Willie's great grandfather, after taking some time to think about it, made the trade.

It was many days later the Navajo learned the truth of the business. The white man had come from the little Mormon community at La Sal Junction, cross-country, heading for his ranch at the northern edge of New Mexico territory—not even a state at the time. He was known to raise horses for a living and bought and sold stock around the La Plata valley. The people down there said he kept good horses and was honest in his trades.

There'd been an unfortunate dalliance with a Mormon woman, the trader told them, and the rancher had barely escaped with his life—leaving half-naked—taking only enough time to empty his pistol at the husband and the woman's brother who came in hot pursuit. The Mormons later told it around that the man only escaped by having a better horse and staying to rough country.

The incensed husband and his brother-in-law thought, for a while, they had him; the Dolores River was in flood at the time and they doubted he could ford it. But he did, somehow, though nearly drowned in the attempt.

His pursuers, being of a more cautious nature, were not so reckless as to follow a desperate man on a good horse across raging waters. They reluctantly gave up the chase and no more was heard of the incident.

Harley had seen that pistol many times—had even shot it as a boy. He hoped his Aunt Willie still had it...along with some cartridges to go with it. Not that there was any danger of anyone finding Eileen, but still...

R. Allen Chappell

11

The Calling

Alfred Nakii wished he could hold out a little longer...maybe give Harley and the woman time to get better situated...but he was exhausted and at the end of his rope, so to speak. He knew this person would not give up and would not leave him alone. *No*, he thought, *this is probably the end.* Alfred could almost visualize his brain swelling inside his skull from that last crack on the head. A black void already hovered above his one working eye, and as he drifted in and out of consciousness, he became even more convinced it was only a matter of time. This person was that dangerous sort he had known in jail; the kind who had nothing left to lose, and was thus capable of doing the worst sort of things. This particular man seemed very good at what he did and wasn't likely to stop until he got what he wanted. He would make him talk eventually; Alfred was sure of it now.

Oh, he knew where the couple was headed all right. They would be going to Harley's people below Tsé Bii' Ndzigaii. That would be the place to hide the woman. *Maybe it wouldn't hurt to tell just that;* it was big country up there and it wasn't likely a stranger could find them in such a place.

Alfred doubted he could take much more. He was almost certain all the fingers on his left hand were now broken, not just torn loose at the joints, but crushed with his own hammer. When the man started on his right hand...that was when he would probably have to tell.

Alfred Nakii was not a weak man, and would not ordinarily have thought anyone could make him tell what he didn't want known, but this stranger was not to be denied; already he had Harley's name and the kind of truck he drove. He was sure the man intended to kill him whether he talked or not. He was beginning to look forward to that—and the quicker the better.

~~~~~~~

Charlie Yazzie and Thomas Begay were in good spirits. It was high time they confronted Harley Ponyboy and let him know they were aware of his new "live in girlfriend," as Thomas referred to the mystery woman. They joked as they drove the considerable distance to Harley's place.

"It must be serious," Charlie grinned. "We haven't seen hide nor hair of him in over a week now."

Thomas chuckled as he pictured the look of dismay on Harley's stout little face when they demanded he fess up. He knew Harley would think it impossible that they had figured it all out for themselves...he had been so careful.

Charlie thought they should just come right out with it—sparing their friend the embarrassment of his subterfuge.

Thomas, on the other hand, preferred Harley should sweat. "We'll make it a payback," he said, "for his underhanded ways." Thomas was enjoying himself. "Why, if it hadn't been for those underwears on the line, he might have gotten away with it. Then God only knows when we would have found out." *It was not the way an old friend conducted himself in such things* was his silent opinion.

As the pair pulled up in Harley Ponyboy's yard, Charlie shut the big Chevy engine off and the two sat studying the place—not willing to credit the absence of a vehicle to mean no one was home.

"No truck?" Charlie murmured.

"That don't mean no one's here; the woman could still be hiding inside, like before." Thomas wasn't one to be discouraged by so slight an indicator as a missing truck. He got down from the Chevy motioning for Charlie to follow.

"Well, there's no underwear on the line this time." Charlie was beginning to think they had wasted a trip.

Thomas, though, was already on the porch, and even before knocking, he tried the doorknob...not really expecting it to swing open. When it did, they were surprised—not about it being unlocked, but rather, that it had been rehung and swung smooth and noiseless. Having been long accustomed to using their shoulder to force the door open they were momentarily caught off guard. The door had been that way since Harley bought the trailer; he often said it was as good as being locked but without the hassle of carrying a key.

Thomas grinned. "You see the difference in having a woman around? There's something to be said for it."

Charlie murmured, "Anita, apparently, was not the right woman to motivate him." He said this with no disrespect and though Thomas knew it was true, he still was a bit put off by the investigator using the woman's name. Harley's ex-wife was just the type whose *chindi* might hop right down to see who was calling it.

Thomas stuck his head inside and called softly. "Anyone here..." And then louder, "Anyone to home?" Both men paused. Listening.

"I guess not." Charlie muttered.

Thomas immediately noticed the new paint and gave the work an approving nod. He admired craftsmanship in any form and thought his friend might have finally acquired the skill of painting—a talent that had eluded him over the years. He moved to the kitchen where he opened the refrigerator to see it virtually barren; other than a few condiments— ketchup mostly—it had been cleaned out. There were three bottles of the red sauce, along with one of mustard and an outdated jar of mayo. He turned to the cupboards and found them equally bare of anything remotely edible. "They didn't even leave a doughnut."

Charlie peered through the open door to the front bedroom and then the closet, also standing open. "It looks to me like they cleared out. There are no women's clothes in this closet."

Thomas, already in the back bedroom, sounded puzzled when he called back. "Harley only has a couple sets of decent clothes to his name and they're gone. There is only his work clothes and some of Anita's old stuff left hanging back here. No sign of the other woman." After a moment or two Thomas emerged from the bedroom looking worried. "The bedding's gone...all the spare blankets along with it." He looked behind the door and frowned when he said, "Harley's old shotgun is gone too. And he always keeps a couple boxes of shells in here with it, but there's none left now. It looks like those two went somewhere they might need a few supplies; from the looks of it, they could be gone a while." His brow furrowed, "Harley must have thought they might need a little protection to take that old shotgun along."

Charlie agreed. "Looks that way all right." He cast a critical eye around the living room. "Everything's nice and neat, though. No sign of being in a rush as far as I can see...almost like they were going on a little camping trip somewhere and planned to be back soon."

The two men moved back out to the porch carefully shutting the door behind them. When they looked at one another, it was plain they were both worried and it showed. Charlie, turning thoughtful now, gazed up the ridge separating Harley's place from that of Alfred Nakii. "Maybe Alfred knows something?"

~~~~~~

Alfred's old pickup truck was pulled right up to the door which now stood ajar. Charlie sounded relieved, "Well at least it looks like Alfred might be at home." Then shook his head, "Doesn't anyone up here ever lock their doors? Alfred, apparently, doesn't even shut his." He smiled. "I guess that's because neither one of them has anything worth stealing and everyone knows it."

Thomas, however, wasn't smiling when he pushed the door open and saw Alfred lying in the middle of the room covered in blood. The couch behind him and even the walls were speckled with gore. Both men immediately thought Harley's neighbor was dead. This caused Thomas to back up a step, and look cautiously around the room, possibly fearing the man's *chindi* could already be hanging around ready to pounce on some unsuspecting innocent.

Charlie edged past the tall *Diné* and stood staring at Alfred Nakii—immobilized by the pitiful sight of a once so familiar person. As he studied the motionless form he thought he detected the flutter of an eyelid and immediately jerked his head toward Thomas. "I think he may still be alive."

The tribal investigator quickly sank to one knee and first tried whispering, but when there was no response, raised his voice. "Alfred, can you hear me?" He put his ear so close it nearly touched the man's swollen lips and asked yet again. Putting a finger on his neck, Charlie thought he detected the vestige of a pulse. "Thomas, get him some water and put something under his head." Charlie was already on his way out the door to the truck and two-way radio. They were high enough here, and close enough to town, that he felt sure he could reach tribal police for an ambulance. Still, he held out very little hope for poor Alfred Nakii. Whoever did this had left him for dead—and Charlie thought this might yet be the case—should help not arrive quickly.

When Charlie returned, Thomas had a sofa pillow under Alfred's head and was holding a cup of water to his lips. "He's trying to say something but I can't quite make it out. He's a tough bastard, Charlie, but he's taken a hell of a beating. If they get someone out here fast enough, though, I think there's still a chance he might make it." He turned his head toward the investigator. "Do you think this has anything to do with Harley and that woman?"

The investigator watched silently from the door; the thought had already occurred to him. This beating of Alfred Nakii *was* more than likely connected to the disappearance of their friend Harley Ponyboy and this mystery woman.

~~~~~~

Thomas Begay paced the hospital corridor while Charlie sat talking quietly to Navajo Policeman Billy Red Clay. The Tribal officer also thought the vicious attack on Alfred Nakii might have something to do with Harley Ponyboy's sudden disappearance. He told Charlie he was meeting with Agent Fred Smith later that morning to hear if the FBI's investigation of the assault might shed further light on the situation. Billy knew it would be days before the official reports were released—but was also aware Agent Smith had a better than average sense of crime scene evaluation and might already have something for them. Crime analysis had been his specialty with the Bureau in Albuquerque and Fred had rightfully earned a reputation for being both perceptive and thorough.

Though Alfred was still in surgery, the doctor on duty made it clear the man's chances of regaining consciousness were not good. "Slim to none…" was his blunt reply when Thomas asked. "The internal bleeding alone is probably enough to kill him…not to mention the head injuries." The doctor had been at the hospital a number of years—worked on a lot of Indians—and admitted he was continually amazed at how tough the people were. He had, more than once, been proven wrong when predicting an Indian wouldn't survive a particular trauma.

Late in the afternoon, Alfred Nakii did indeed rally, but only for a short while. Captain Beyale of Navajo Police had assigned a man to stay by his bedside in case he came around; the officer told them Alfred could only mumble a little before, again, lapsing into unconsciousness. Unfortunately, the policeman was unable to make sense of what few words he could make out.

The doctor, for his part, thought it remarkable Alfred had hung on even this long, but still felt there was little hope.

When word of what happened got around—and on the reservation these things always get around—Charlie Yazzie put the word out he would like to hear from anyone who might have anything helpful concerning Alfred Nakii. Within hours he received a call from a former client of Legal Services. Charlie had once intervened for the woman in a spousal abuse case. She was now determined to repay that kindness. She said she had seen Alfred Nakii in the Social Club only the day before and heard him in conversation with another customer. The two of them were talking about some woman with red hair. Charlie's interest was piqued at once; his client had worked part time at Rosie's for a long time and in their previous dealings, he'd found her to be reliable.

The other man, the barmaid said, seemed especially intrigued when he noticed Alfred became nervous at the mention of the woman with the red hair (the same woman, she thought, that Rosie Johnson was spreading the word about only days before). After Alfred left the bar, the man mentioned to her Alfred seemed to know something about the red-haired woman. The man said he intended talking to Rosie—thinking it might be nice to have that reward.

When Charlie brought this up to Billy Red Clay, the young officer immediately showed an interest, and after thinking a minute said, "Maybe Fred Smith would consider going along with us on this one." He then smiled. "The FBI carries a little more authority in town than we do."

Charlie thought about this, nodded, and allowed Billy was probably right. He didn't ask to take Thomas Begay along this time, though the thought had previously crossed his mind. He knew that would be pressing his luck.

Agent Smith agreed to meet them at the Social Club in an hour, and Charlie checked his watch thinking they could just make it.

~~~~~~~~

When Charlie and Billy pulled up in front of the bar, the FBI man's plain grey sedan with government plates was glaringly obvious to those inside. As the denizens of the seedy bar considered the impending incursion, there came a hurried exit of shifty-eyed patrons, most of whom avoided eye contact as they quickly disappeared up the street.

Billy Red Clay smiled at Fred as the agent got out of his car and gave him a quick salute.

Charlie Yazzie lifted a hand as well and figured the FBI man must have intended making just such an impression.

The pair joined Fred on the sidewalk—watching intently as several more drinkers left the bar in search of less intimidating watering holes.

Fred immediately made mention of the fact that his junior agent hadn't been able to get much out of the bar owner...or her patrons...when he was last there investigating Benny Klees's abandoned pickup. Several days had passed and still no witnesses had come forward to say who might have left the truck.

"No," Billy said, "I don't imagine your man had any luck down here, and I doubt I'd have done much better myself. These people don't trust *any* law." Billy frowned at the placard in the window of the lounge. "We may not find it any easier today."

"We'll see." Fred had a little smile on his face, but there was no smile in his eyes. He had the look of someone who meant business and knew exactly how that business should be handled.

"I hear Rosie doesn't like her customers being harassed," Charlie Yazzie offered. "I'd say we should have her full attention by now. Thomas says she's an in-your-face sort who won't hesitate to confront the law," adding cautiously, "regardless of what badge they carry."

Now it was Billy's turn to smile. "From what I hear, Sheriff Dudd Schott won't even bother coming down here anymore."

Charlie grinned. "And with good reason too. The Sheriff wore out his welcome here when he was still a deputy." Both men waited, expecting to see the FBI man look more concerned.

Fred Smith, however, gave no notice he'd heard any of this and if intimidated in any way, he didn't show it.

The lounge was dark inside, smelling of old cigarette smoke and stale beer. The afternoon crowd of regulars had just been gathering when the entourage of officials from three different agencies unceremoniously descended on the establishment.

Though it was broad daylight outside, there was hardly enough light in the bar to recognize faces, which was the way the clientele preferred it. Rosie's customers favored anonymity...even toward each other.

Charlie had never been in the place, but even he had to smile at the big Indian chief's picture over the bar. He nudged Billy Red Clay, indicating the picture with a push of his lips, an uncharacteristic gesture for the Legal Services investigator. Billy Red Clay chuckled as he read the inscription: "We have reservations!"

Fred Smith followed their gaze…but seemed not to get what the picture was about…or if he did, he didn't let on.

Rosie wasn't behind the bar, but Charlie's informant was, and she cautiously looked them over before making her way down to wipe a clean spot for them.

"Is Rosie Johnson here?" The FBI man sounded quite businesslike, as he flashed his I.D, causing the woman to raise an eyebrow at Charlie Yazzie; she hadn't counted on the Feds being involved and was now obviously rethinking her previous offer to help; she thought she would be dealing only with the Tribal investigator.

The barmaid was clearly apprehensive and side-eyed Charlie, as she inspected the agent's credentials "She just went to the back. I can get her if you want?"

Charlie, seeing his former client becoming more than a little nervous, motioned her over. "We aren't going to involve you in this…won't mention you at all in fact." This seemed to lessen the woman's concern and she appeared slightly more at ease as she hurried to fetch her boss—for what she now hoped would be a routine questioning—one leaving her out of it, as Charlie had promised.

It was less than a minute before the lounge owner blustered through the office door and stomped her way down the bar to glare at the three men. "I've already told you people everything I know about that pickup truck…which is nothing!" Her eyes darted from one to the other and there was no worry or nervousness about her as she slammed the flat of her great paw on the bar in front of them."

Fred Smith, despite his innocuous appearance, calmly flashed his badge, set his jaw, and leaned forward—almost nose to nose with the big woman. He growled, "We're not here about the truck," causing the big woman to rock back momentarily and reconsider her attitude. The Feds were the Feds after all, and this one had his game face on.

Billy Red Clay stood back and watched, hoping to learn something he might someday use to his own advantage; still he remained ready to jump in should the situation warrant it.

Charlie, for his part, only crossed his arms and tried to look as stern as possible, hoping the other officers would at least take that as a show of solidarity.

The FBI Agent let his eyes wander about the lounge, giving the impression he was taking in the most minute of details. He focused a critical glance at the back bar where the establishment's licenses were displayed, studied them a moment, then turned his attention to the lighting and electrical fixtures. Finally, the lawman glared. "I see at least three violations of local and federal statutes that put you in noncompliance, Ms. Johnson." Fred's gaze did not waver in the least and he now spoke in a threatening tone of his own. "I can shut you down and keep you shut down for a long while...and I will... make no mistake about that, Rosie."

Charlie Yazzie glanced about—wondering what the agent could possibly have seen to warrant such accusations. He was, nonetheless, left with the distinct impression Agent Smith could, and would, stand behind those allegations—regardless of what Rosie Johnson might think to the contrary. This is what made the FBI...the FBI. Their training was known the world over to be without peer when it came to the procedurals of modern law enforcement.

Establishing some sort of psychological high ground was an obvious priority for Agent Smith and he was not yet through. "Then, Rosie...there's the more urgent matter of withholding information in a homicide investigation...possibly two homicides, in fact. This could get nasty...and fast."

This talk of *two* homicides surprised both Billy Red Clay and Charlie Yazzie—leaving both men wondering what Agent Smith meant by *two* homicides.

Rosie, for her part, was fast coming to the conclusion she may have misjudged the severity of the situation. She was now thinking any perceived involvement might exact a price she was unwilling to pay. She had no doubt Federal Agent Smith was a bulldog. He had taken hold and wasn't going to let go until he got what he wanted. Rosie became even more doubtful she could justify the consequences this federal agent had so clearly laid out. Her demeanor, bold though it first had been, paled considerably, and her icy resolve, for the first time in years, showed signs of melting.

"Well, look here now." The big woman's protest turned wheedling and she looked from one to the other for some sign of consideration—then caught herself as she glanced down the length of the bar to make sure no one had overheard or taken notice. It would not do to show any sort of weakness or cooperation with the law—not in this business, it wouldn't.

"Come on back to the office," she finally muttered, leading the way.

After nearly forty-five minutes of intensive interrogation, the three lawmen were convinced Rosie Johnson had at last told them what she knew about this stranger making inquiries into the woman with red hair. The man had taken the room she sometimes rented, she said, and paid up for three days before moving out the next night without even asking for a refund. When she showed them upstairs to the room, Fred Smith cautioned her to keep it locked after they left and to not allow anyone inside until his forensic team got there.

Billy Red Clay and Charlie Yazzie stayed outside the door, only peering inside, as Fred took the few steps to the middle of the room. The agent did a slow turn of the shabby accommodations, leaving the two Navajo with the impression he had missed nothing. He nodded again to himself, turned to leave, and then smiled at the two, yet said nothing.

Billy, nonetheless, felt the agent had learned something of value, and remained in awe of his perceived investigative prowess. Billy thought his own agency should fall into better compliance with FBI protocol, and meant to bring it up in the next Interagency Meeting—not that he hadn't mentioned it before—but his resolve was now strengthened in that direction.

Later, Fred would tell the pair he was almost certain his people would find prints. "It's easier to wipe down a pickup than it is an entire room, especially a dirty room...not many are able to do it without missing the odd print or two. If this is the same man we think he is, he may well have been in more of a hurry this time and not taken such care as before." There was something else the agent had noticed but kept this information to himself for the time being; on the little table beside the bed was a Gideon Bible and peeking out from inside it—a blue, silk bookmark.

Charlie was somewhat mollified that the FBI now considered this stranger a prime suspect in the murder of the old silversmith from Teec Nos Pos. Fred Smith probably thought so from the start, and this served to increase Charlie's respect for the agent...and for his agency. He and Thomas Begay felt, from the beginning, the man should be a prime suspect, and he was pleased to see they had been vindicated in that assumption. Still, he wished the Bureau had seen fit to confer that information a little earlier on.

That a murderer would make so bold as to take a room, right there at Rosie's, after abandoning the victim's truck nearby was a ruse that nearly worked— yet another indicator of the fugitive's sly but twisted mental state. Charlie had to admit the brazen act served its purpose.

No one could know how closely all their fates were now entwined, nor could they know how their lives would be even more violently impacted.

12

The Quest

It was an anxious Harley Ponyboy that slowed his truck and pulled to the side of the road to gaze up the hill at Lucy Tallwoman's camp. On his way back to town it occurred to him he might save time by borrowing Lucy's new telephone, maybe even catch Charlie Yazzie at his office. He was certain Charlie was now his best chance for help. The Legal Services investigator was, in fact, the only official he trusted to understand Eileen's dilemma.

Harley was obsessed with the thought that Eileen, left in such unfamiliar surroundings as his Aunt Willie's, might become stressed to the point of doing something so foolish as leave the security of his family's camp. As desperate as she might believe her situation to be, he knew she was at least as safe there, for the time being, as she would be anywhere else. His Aunt Willie had family and clan scattered all over that area, and should push come to shove, those people would provide an extra barrier of protection.

Family still looked out for each other in that part of the country.

As he made his way up the one-lane track to Lucy Tallwoman's newly built house, he didn't see Thomas's truck in front, but still hoped to find it parked out back next to Paul T'Sosi's old hogan. Thomas often left it there to take advantage of the little patch of shade the new house provided. The truck's blue paint was newer than the vehicle itself and Thomas intended to keep it that way as long as possible.

Harley drove around the corner of the building—there still was no vehicle in sight. He stopped to consider but before he could think what to do next, the door of the hogan swung open and Paul T'Sosi appeared looking either surprised...or possibly... agitated at the sight of him. The old man hesitated only a moment then motioned for him to follow as he headed for the back door of the house.

Harley frowned, but got down from the truck and hurried toward the open door where he saw Paul already taking a pot of coffee from the stove. The old man didn't ask; just brought two cups and the pot over to the table. He pushed his chin toward a chair then pulled out one for himself. There was a can of evaporated milk along with a sugar bowl next to a glass of spoons. Paul poured the cups three-quarters full, leaving room for the required dollop of canned milk and several spoons of sugar.

The old singer didn't waste time with niceties. "Where you been, Harley? Everybody in the country has been looking for you." The old man waited, eyes flat, a frown pulling at the corners of his mouth.

R. Allen Chappell

Harley stirred his coffee before looking up. "Now, why would anyone be lookin' for me, Paul?"

"Well, I guess, because they wondered if you might be dead, too, like Alfred Nakii...he died about an hour ago. Thomas and Lucy were up at the hospital. Charlie Yazzie was there, too."

Harley appeared unmoved by this news as though he hadn't heard Paul, or if he had, didn't understand what he was saying; he only shook his head at the old man. "No, Paul. I just talked to Alfred this morning and he was fine. Alfred's not dead."

"Well, Harley, he may have been fine this morning, but he is sure dead now. Lucy told me she and Thomas were with him when he died. And from what they could figure, they thought you might be dead too." Paul blew on his coffee before taking a long slow sip. "My daughter said someone might be out to get you because of some woman." The old man stared directly at Harley Ponyboy knowing full well it was bad manners, but not caring. The old singer wasn't often so rude. "For a while they thought Alfred might make it...be able tell them what happened." The old man looked at his cup, made a sour face, and stirred in another spoon of sugar. "I guess he did come around a time or two all right, but only for a minute each time...so badly beaten he couldn't say much. The doctor told them something was torn loose inside. No one understood the word he used but he made it plain it was something he couldn't fix. He told them, then, Alfred probably wouldn't make it."

Paul paused a moment and thought back to the call from his daughter. "The doc even sent the cop away...telling him Alfred was about done and

138

wouldn't wake up again." The old man forced a half-smile. "But he didn't know Alfred." He gazed off into the distance, "Our family always liked that boy...we been knowing his mother a long time. Even with Alfred being in jail, she still thought he would make some woman a good husband...she never stopped looking. 'It would have to be someone special, who could keep a tight rein on him,' she would say. 'Help him stay out of trouble,' she told everyone. His momma was certain that person would come along one day...thought so right up to the time she died...hoping for those grandbabies she was always talking about, I guess."

Harley worried through this talk, but was not quite willing to believe Alfred was gone. It was only after listening to Paul a while longer that he slowly came to the realization *Alfred must be dead.* Harley, too, then went to the sugar bowl and dumped another spoonful in his coffee, stirring it absentmindedly for nearly a minute before asking, "Who killed him?" His shoulders had taken a slump, as though he already knew. He sat back in his chair with a growing premonition *he* was the cause of his friend's horrific end.

"That's what they still don't know, Harley, but Lucy let on it might have something to do with that woman you been hiding out. That's what they think––you been hiding someone's woman up at your place. Whoever's looking for her probably beat Alfred to death trying to find out where you two were." Paul didn't say this in an accusatory manner but that was, nonetheless, the way it came across to Harley Ponyboy, and in his mind, it reinforced his growing sense of guilt.

Harley had a way of thinking bad things were just naturally his fault…even when they weren't. Professor Custer had once supposed the little man might have developed a guilt complex after Anita's death. Then, too, there was the drinking that came after—*that* hadn't helped. He suggested to Harley he seek professional help. Harley took this to mean Old Man Paul T'Sosi who he had long considered his go-to medical consultant for mental or physical ills.

The old singer, though thinking himself retired, had risen to the occasion and studied long and hard to find the proper rite or ceremony that could help; but nothing, so far, had worked. He was certain now; the problem had something to do with Harley's *hozo* being out of whack. He had performed several ceremonies he thought might fix the problem, but still nothing came of it. Finally, Paul had to admit his friend might have to look elsewhere for relief.

"Harley, Alfred's death isn't something you knowingly caused, and I don't think anyone is saying it was." Paul hesitated, as Harley sat nervously clearing his throat, and then went on to tell him the rest of what happened at the hospital. "When Alfred recovered consciousness for the last time, he whispered something about telling where you were hiding. He couldn't remember for sure, he said, but thought he might have told that man where you were heading." Nearly choking on his next words, the old man forced himself to continue, "Just before he died, Alfred said, 'Someone should warn Harley.' " Paul's voice grew softer. "Those were his last words, too."

This didn't make Harley feel any better, and he rose from his chair saying, "I need to get with Charlie and figure out what ta do. That man might already be on his way up there."

"Lucy said Thomas and Charlie were thinking the same thing; she said those boys were going to stop by here before heading on up to that country west of *Tsé Bii' Ndzisgaii*. Thomas knows where your Aunt Willie lives up there." Paul held up a finger to emphasize his next point. "That was nearly an hour ago. They should be getting here any minute now." Seeing the doubtful look on Harley's face, Paul threw up his hands. "Call Sue Yazzie. She should be home now. She'll tell you." He threw his hands in the air again. "Call her up if you don't believe me."

Harley was on his way to the phone before the old man finished speaking. He knew the number by heart, and while he didn't have a phone himself, he had memorized the numbers for Thomas Begay and Charlie Yazzie. Those were the only two people he personally knew who had telephones.

Sue sounded out of breath when she answered, but relieved to hear it was Harley on the line. "Yes, Thomas and Charlie are headed up your way... probably be there in just a few minutes. Lucy might take a while longer; she had to stop by the store for some things they might need." Before hanging up, Sue was adamant when she said, "Harley, don't do anything silly—wait for Charlie, he'll know what to do about this."

When Harley hung up, he was still determined to be on his way back up toward Monument Valley.

Now that he knew help was on the way, he suddenly became terrified Claude Bell might somehow run across one of his clansmen up there and treat them the way he had Alfred Nakii. True, it was big country, but according to Eileen, this Claude Bell was a resourceful and vicious man capable of anything.

Paul T'Sosie remained silent as he watched Harley come back to the kitchen. He could see the little man was even more distraught and still on the verge of leaving. Paul focused on talking him out of it, and again tried reasoning with him, "It will only be a few minutes until there are people here to help you Harley. It would be foolish to go it alone when they are so close." Then he threw out the clincher. "You need Charlie up there so you have the law on your side. Charlie's smart and so is Thomas…at least when it comes to this sort of thing." Paul was never overly generous when it came to praising Thomas Begay— in spite of the fact the two had been getting along well the last year or so. Paul had a long memory when it came to those things he chose not to let go.

13

The Investigation

Billy Red Clay sat in his tiny office looking over the latest folder from Fred Smith at the FBI; this one was the autopsy report on Gilbert Nez. Billy's interest in the case had grown. Curiosity, maybe, plus the fact the man was, after all, related. There were two points Billy kept coming back to. Number one: the blue silk bookmark among his clansman's meager possessions. He doubted Gilbert had been much of a reader, Bible or otherwise, and it appeared the bookmark was identical to the one found in old Benny Klee's abandoned pickup truck.

The second thing that caught Billy's attention was a short note toward the end of the autopsy folder, jotted in the margin of the last page. It appeared to be no more than an afterthought, which only made it more conspicuous to the young policeman. Despite the fact the death was officially attributed to a heart attack, the forensics technician examining the blood samples apparently found certain indicators of suffocation—not enough to cause death certainly—but enough to precipitate the heart attack listed as the primary cause of death. Billy flipped back through the report. There were no marks of strangulation, nor was there evidence of any other mark of violence beyond the usual small scratches and bruises one would likely find on any indigent or homeless person. It was a rough life out there for such people. And Billy Red Clay knew it to be one that accrued its share of battle wounds.

Billy was not yet born when Gilbert Nez left the reservation, for what he thought would be a more exciting life. In fact, Billy had never seen the man growing up...except in photos. He recalled one in particular: a shot of Gilbert holding his Uncle Thomas when Thomas was a boy, likely no more than four or five years old. Both were smiling: Thomas looking up at Gilbert, possibly thinking *this is the way it will always be*.

The only other picture was the medical examiner's decidedly morbid autopsy shot. Billy looked again at the photo attachment on the inside cover of the folder. Even in death, he could see the resemblance between father and son.

Gilbert Nez's frequent absences, and later mistreatment of his wife and child, had caused Thomas's mother to give her son her own family's name...Begay. Gilbert's half-brother at Navajo Mountain, John Nez, had taken this in stride though the bulk of responsibility for Thomas's upbringing would now fall to him—a common tradition among the Navajo. John, had, in fact, remained the central male figure in the boy's early years and still played an important role in Thomas's life. The elder Nez was the polar opposite of his brother, Gilbert. John Nez, now on the Tribal Council, had become a man respected in his community—being married to a white woman had not diminished his standing in the least. His wife Marissa, an anthropologist affiliated with a prominent university, now continued her work from the vantage point of an insider and was the envy of many of her peers.

Billy Red Clay wondered if he shouldn't just let this entire Gilbert Nez thing pass, for what most conceded was a natural death—the death of a person who no longer mattered to anyone.

We'll see what Fred Smith has to say about it, Billy told himself, as he gathered up his hat and sidearm. He turned and shook his head as he looked around his cubbyhole of an office, wondering how long it would take until he could wrangle an office like Charlie Yazzie's. He was nearly to his unit when FBI Agent Fred Smith, himself, pulled into the parking lot, and spotting the Navajo policeman, changed course to intercept him.

"How are you Billy?" The agent smiled, rolling down the window as he pulled into the space next to the policeman's. "You are just the guy I wanted to see."

Billy came up to the agent's car thinking nothing looked so official, or intimidating, as a plain, unmarked vehicle with government license plates and a two-way antenna—the average person took it to mean very serious business indeed.

"Well, I'm glad you caught me, Fred. I was just going over the report you sent on Gilbert Nez. Thanks for that, by the way." The Navajo policeman hesitated, considering the matter he really wanted to go over with the agent. "I was just on my way to see Charlie Yazzie. I'm sure you're already aware of the

Alfred Nakii assault. More than that now, I'm afraid. Charlie just called to tell me he passed away only a short time ago."

The FBI man shut off his engine. "That's why I'm here, actually. I was on my way to lunch when the call came through to the office." The agent grimaced as he eased himself out of the car, obviously favoring one leg. "Fell off my son's bike yesterday; I was trying to show him how to turn without having a wreck...when I had one." Both men grinned as Agent Smith held out an official looking manila folder.

"Oh, what's this about?" Billy frowned. "Not something I screwed up, I hope."

"No, no...not at all. Just had this in from the lab this morning and thought you might like a little heads-up. It's the results from our little foray down to Rosie's place; Albuquerque's take on some of what our boys found. When we were going over the suspect's room, I noticed something I thought needed more clarification than we were able to implement at the time."

Billy took the folder he was handed but didn't bother opening it. He knew Fred intended to say more, and didn't want to miss the agent's personal take on the report. He preferred hearing it firsthand; he could read the actual report later. In Billy's experience the nuances of the spoken word often told more than the dry wording of an official report. A lift of his chin encouraged Fred to continue.

Smith smiled at this common Navajo tactic. He learned, early on, that many *Diné* gain a greater understanding from a personal interaction as opposed to reading that same information. Over the years Fred had developed a good knowledge of how the *Diné* process information, he'd grown up with them and his thinking in that regard had been formed at an early age. His grandfather was a trader to the Navajo and Fred spent a good bit of his summer vacations working at the trading post in that isolated stretch between Bloomfield and Cuba, New Mexico. This was the primary difference between Smith and the former agent in charge—Fred understood the Navajo.

"On the bedside table in the suspect's room at Rosie's, I was pretty sure the bookmarker I saw in that Bible was the same as the previous two we turned up; the one in Benny Klee's pickup, and the other one the coroner found on Gilbert Nez. I thought it was about time we took a closer look at them. There's obviously a correlation there somewhere." The agent shrugged. "The Sheriff's Office still maintains they're most likely handouts from a local religious canvasser. But they have not, so far, been able to make that connection. Sheriff Schott says they're still looking." Both lawmen smiled at this.

Fred Smith gave a dismissive wave of his hand before going on. "Our lab did say the items were identical in manufacture. It didn't take our people long to find where they were from. The Phoenix Bible Outreach Center runs a rehab organization—drug and alcohol addiction mainly. They recently had a team leader attacked and killed; authorities suspect a parolee in their program may be responsible. There was an eyewitness according to the center's director, but both she and the supposed murderer have disappeared. No one is sure what part the woman played in the murder...if any."

Billy wondered out loud, "So you think one or both of these people are responsible for the Klee murder?"

The FBI Agent shook his head, and frowned at the folder in Billy's hand, before going on. "We, of course, immediately verified all of this information with our Phoenix office. The alleged attacker is a real bad boy with a serious rap sheet to his credit, including at least two priors involving murder, already to his credit. Prosecutors, so far, seem unable to bring homicide charges that will stick—mainly because witnesses seem to turn up dead before they can testify. One witness, a former partner of the suspect and a fellow inmate in a Federal Corrections Center, was found murdered in his cell." Fred stopped for a moment to consider if he'd covered everything and then debated how best to fill the liaison officer in on something that wasn't mentioned in the report.

"You do understand, Billy, what I'm about to tell you has not been cleared for official release, and definitely is not for local dissemination, at least not yet. This is strictly between you and me for the time being." The agent winced, as he shifted his weight to his good leg, and rubbed the injured knee for a moment before going on. "The suspect's name is Claude Bell. He's thought to be accompanied by a female companion; a small, younger looking woman, possibly with red hair, and also from the Rehab Center. Her name is Eileen May and she is part Navajo. The woman seems to have no priors beyond a DUI and one or two public drunkenness charges. The Bible center's director claims she was a model participant in their program and was there, apparently, of her own volition. She was scheduled to complete the program in only a few more weeks and then be sponsored by an aunt in Utah."

Billy Red Clay was taking all this in, but couldn't help wondering where it was going.

Agent Smith shifted back and forth from one leg to the other, testing the bad knee, then frowned and went on. "I guess the bottom line is...the director doesn't think it likely she would take up with Bell of her own accord. She was one of their top Bible salesmen and apparently well liked by her fellow team members." Here the FBI man leaned back against his car slightly to ease the obviously increasing discomfort of the knee. "The director believes this Bell character may have taken her against her will. An elderly area resident told investigators she spotted the pair driving off in the woman's car not long after she heard sirens at the Center." Fred Smith shook his head and held up a hand to signal he was finished. "I'm going to go get this knee wrapped, Billy. It's really starting to hurt."

The Navajo policeman gave the agent's leg a sympathetic nod and then stood watching him pull out. All he could think of was the death of Gilbert Nez. This Claude Bell was in the same area at the same time Gilbert was at Rosie's. Bell might even have been watching from his room above the bar. Or the owner may have tipped him off when Thomas was talking to Gilbert. In either case, he might well have followed the old man on the off chance he knew something about the woman. For Gilbert Nez, this chance encounter with his son might have led to his death.

14

Up Country

Harley Ponyboy waited nearly twenty minutes for Thomas Begay and Charlie Yazzie before jumping in his truck, and despite old man Paul T'Sosi's entreaties, turned toward the highway where he was out of sight before the old man finished cussing.

It was clear to Harley his friends had been somehow delayed, or perhaps decided to head directly up to Monument Valley without stopping by Thomas's place. To his mind there was no telling when, or even if, they would show up. After hearing about Alfred Nakii, he knew time was no longer on his side. There would have to be a new plan—a different place for Eileen and him to hide—and it had to happen now.

The sandstone spires were already throwing long shadows as he turned west off the highway toward his Aunt Willie's camp. Harley hoped it hadn't been too depressing for Eileen out there. It had only been a day but he suspected she might already be growing anxious. Hopefully missing *him* was part of that. He thought the recent turn her life had taken was enough to make anyone depressed. He was, in fact, becoming depressed himself just thinking about it. As he neared the second turnoff, he saw a person standing by the road. The boy—the one seen herding sheep earlier that morning—waved him down. When Harley pulled over, he could see the youngster had been crying, but was wiping his face on a sleeve to prevent Harley from noticing.

"Is everything all right here?" Harley glanced across at the hogan, saw no vehicle in sight, nor did he see any sign of the old man and woman that had been there that morning. "Where are your people?" He asked in Navajo, thinking that might be the reason the boy wasn't answering. He figured the boy to be no more than nine or ten years old.

He could see the child was doing his best to control his voice. "I...I can't find my grandfather or grandmother," he finally choked out. "They weren't here when I brought the sheep home. The truck's gone, too. They never, both of them, been gone at the same time." He wiped his nose again before going on. "My grandfather can't see good enough to drive—too old to drive anymore." The boy looked off down the road, "I don't know why they would leave me here?"

Harley thought for a moment the boy might start crying again. "Well, maybe they just went into town to get groceries or something." He was having another premonition this might be just the start of bigger problems...for both of them.

"No, they just went shopping two days ago. They only go to town every couple weeks, sometimes only once a month." The boy again sniffled a time or two then caught his breath with a quick gulp. "My grandmother says she can't take those bumpy roads more than that. She's the one that has to drive."

Harley was not quite sure what to do; he couldn't leave the boy alone out here in his present state, not with night coming on. But it was urgent he get on up to Willie's and make sure *they* were all right. The boy's people, after all, might have just run down the road to a neighbor's, or perhaps one had fallen ill, or been injured somehow and needed to go in for medical attention. There was probably a perfectly logical explanation. In his heart, however, Harley Ponyboy knew it might be something far more sinister. *If I take the boy with me and the old people show back up, they won't know where he is and that would be worse.* Harley looked again at the boy and finally shook his head as he motioned for the youngster to get in the truck.

The boy, sensing what was coming, had taken a step back—immediately declaring he couldn't leave the sheep by themselves. They had been having trouble with coyotes, he said, and their dog was going to have puppies soon—she couldn't fight them off by herself. They'd had a big male coyote get in the corral only the night before, but had heard the commotion and his grandfather scared it off before it could do any harm to the sheep...or the dog.

Harley knew exactly how this boy was thinking; he had herded sheep in this country himself and probably around the same age. Those sheep were the boy's responsibility, and quite probably, all his family had of any value. The boy knew he was the only one left to make sure nothing happened to them. That's just how it was out here on the *Diné Bikeyah*.

Harley slowly came to a decision: he nodded and reached up to the gun rack in the rear window, passing the boy his old shotgun. "Do you know how to shoot this?"

The boy gave the shotgun a cursory look, saw nothing he didn't already know about, and nodding back, took the handful of shells Harley offered; then turned and started back toward the hogan.

"Hey," Harley called. "What is your name?"

"My name is Arnold... Arnold T'si."

"Arnold, there should be some friends of mine along pretty soon in a white Chevy pickup with a Tribal emblem on the door. It will look like the police, but they are not policemen; they are coming to help me. Keep an eye out for them and when you see them coming—flag them down. They have a two-way radio and will call in some help for you, and check on your people too." Harley held a finger in the air, shaking it for emphasis, "Tell them Harley Ponyboy is up at Willie Etcitty's place in Yellow Canyon. Someone will come back by here later on to check on you so don't worry." With this Harley put his truck in gear and pointed it up the long grade to the side canyon where he'd left Eileen May. He felt bad about leaving the boy alone but thought it wouldn't be for long. Still the nagging worry of Arnold T'si, and his grandparents, added to his torment. He feared their situation might be a precursor of things to come.

Harley had gone only a few miles when he came upon his Aunt Willie's battered Jeep pickup, nosed over in the ditch, the hood up and driver's door ajar. He pulled to one side and cautiously approached the abandoned vehicle. There was only one set of tracks leaving the driver's side—the small slender tracks of a woman. The prints led down country toward the

153

highway. He could see through the open truck door that the key was still in the ignition and had been left turned on. The gas gauge showed empty, making it obvious the truck had run out of gas leaving the driver afoot. That might explain the disappearance of the old couple and their vehicle; they were the first camp on the way out to the highway. Harley, even while confronting the evidence, had a hard time bringing himself to believe it was Eileen.

~~~~~~

Charlie Yazzie thought it foolish of Harley not to have waited there at Lucy Tallwoman's camp, knowing full well he and Thomas Begay were on their way out there.

Thomas Begay was of the opinion, their friend's mind was affected by this new woman in his life, and he didn't hesitate to say so. "Harley's not thinking straight—this woman has him all screwed up—maybe she has put a spell on him."

Mentally dismissing the part about the spell, Charlie still thought there was more to it than just the woman. "I doubt this is all about her. I'm pretty sure Harley's feeling some guilt over Alfred Nakii, too." Charlie had no doubt Harley was taking the news of Alfred's tortured death in the worst possible way.

Old man Paul T'Sosie looked on as though in a daze and could only watch as Thomas began gathering what he thought they might need in that isolated area west of Monument Valley. Charlie stayed in the truck talking via radio to Tribal Officer Billy Red Clay—now on his way back from a prisoner delivery to Window Rock. Billy made it plain his department was spread pretty thin at the moment, but he would try to catch up with them somewhere up in the *Tsé Bii' Ndzisgaii* country.

Charlie's unofficial hunt was now focused on finding Harley Ponyboy, who, he now felt certain, was sheltering the missing woman, putting her under the protection of family and clan, and possibly endangering all of them.

Billy, more interested in the murder suspect Claude Bell, agreed that Harley and the woman might cause the fugitive to show himself at some point. Still the liaison officer was quick to point out: "There is still the matter of the FBI's right of jurisdiction. We can't cross the Bureau on this one, Charlie," he cautioned. "I have a call in to Agent Smith as we speak, but I haven't heard back as yet. Fred will get back to us ...I'm just not sure when."

Charlie could tell Billy Red Clay didn't intend to make an official move on any of this without a go-ahead from the Bureau—not that he blamed him. It was Billy's neck on the line. He knew the young policeman had always envied Charlie's autonomy at Legal Services, including his greater latitude in decision-making. *There is something to be said for having a law degree* Charlie thought, though he was well aware there was more to it than just that.

Paul T'Sosi had put some sandwiches and drinks together for them and was obviously waiting to be asked along. When that didn't happen, he watched the proceedings with less enthusiasm and didn't follow them out to the truck when they left.

Once on the road, Thomas sat slouched against the passenger side door. He hadn't slept well the previous night and doubted Charlie had either.

"Helluva thing about Alfred Nakii...I guess you're right about Harley; he must be feeling pretty bad about Alfred's death. The little guy probably believes he's responsible. He'll just naturally think it's all his fault." Thomas closed one eye at the endless stretch of highway. "Which I guess it is, when you stop to think about it."

Charlie nodded. "I'm surprised he didn't stick around down there with Paul...maybe take advantage of another cleansing ceremony." He said this without his usual degree of frustration over Harley's predilection for traditional medicine. *Everyone needs to believe in something, I guess. Hell, I don't even know what I believe in anymore.*

Charlie had gone from an old-fashioned cultural upbringing to the gradual rejection of most of those same traditional beliefs. He was beginning to understand how much had been lost during that time at boarding school, and then university, and though he felt no real regret, there still was an empty place inside when he thought about it. Charlie had noticed of late, however, the longer he was back among his more traditional friends and relatives, the more sense some of those cultural beliefs actually made. He could see now how many of those myths and superstitions evolved—some of them over thousands of years—all to answer the needs of a people trying to survive. He was coming to the realization a person didn't have to go 'back to the blanket' to have an appreciation of his own culture.

~~~~~~~

As Harley Ponyboy approached his Aunt Willie's camp, he saw her come outside, shade her eyes with a hand, and then break into a shuffling run as she recognized his truck. Her old father followed—talking to himself and shaking his cane in the air. The two were plainly upset and it didn't take long to find out why.

"That woman stole our truck!" The old man shouted before even saying hello. His recent wife-hunting expedition had gone badly and he was in no mood to be nice to his clan nephew who, he felt, was responsible for bringing a thief to their door.

Aunt Willie stopped and turned to admonish her father in Navajo. "If you don't slow down and calm yourself you might fall and break something...and then where will you be, old man?" When she returned her attention to Harley, he could see she, too, was more than a little distraught at this betrayal by a guest. She spoke Navajo, and her voice rose as she continued. "We were taking a nap—then when we woke up—the truck was gone. That woman must have let it roll back down the road a good piece before starting it up. We never did hear anything." She frowned at Harley. "What sort of woman have you taken up with, Nephew?"

"Now, Auntie, I found your truck off in a ditch just down the road. Let's not be too quick to think badly of Eileen. She may have become frightened and thought she needed to get away from here. She has some troubles following her—maybe she had some sign that trouble was getting close and didn't want to get you mixed up in it."

"Humph…" Willie nodded reluctantly, and then admitted her friend Elma had come by that morning on her way to get wood. "She was saying her neighbor down country ran across a stranger asking questions about a woman; the woman was his sister, he told Elma, but she didn't believe him. She said he was the type of person no one would want looking for them anyway, sister or not." Willie seemed to be putting these things together in her head, slowly becoming less critical of Eileen.

"Elma never saw Eileen—she stayed in the hogan and didn't come out. We didn't say anything about her and Elma never knew she was here." Willie's face softened toward her nephew, and she was about to ask if he wanted coffee, when her father, not hearing any of their conversation, came right up to Harley and he thought for a moment the old man was going to give him a whack with his cane; it would not be the first time either. Many years before, when Harley was yet a teenager, Grover had discovered him and two other cousins drinking a pint of whiskey in the arroyo below his grandmother's camp. He'd commenced whaling them with that very cane. He then took the further trouble to look up their eldest cousin: the one who had given them the liquor. Grover gave *him* a couple of good whacks as well. It caused a lot of trouble in the family and for weeks afterward no one said much about the affair…or even spoke to one another at all, for that matter. None of this, however, dissuaded Harley from drinking whenever he got the chance.

Later, when Harley's family moved to town, and he started hanging out with Thomas Begay; the die was cast and it was all downhill from there.

Harley figured the old man was now too feeble to do much harm with his stick but still eyed him uneasily, thinking he might have to take the cane away from him.

"Now, Grandfather," Harley addressed him using the familiar clan term for an elder. "Try to be reasonable. Nothing good can come of you hitting me with that stick..." But the old man held his threatening stance and still might have made a move, had it not been for his daughter. It was Willie who finally took the cane from her father and shushed him in the Navajo way—more of a hiss than anything else.

"You two should apologize to each other." Willie looked from one to the other and stomped her foot so they could see how upset she was. "I won't stand for this foolishness...not in my own camp."

The old man pouted but finally dropped his head and apologized, though his voice was so low it could barely be heard.

Harley, too, sighed and apologized, but wasn't quite sure what he was apologizing for at this point. He understood the old man was upset about the truck, but still thought Grover was blowing the thing all out of proportion. The truck was okay—at least he thought it would be after they pulled it out of the ditch.

Willie, now satisfied each was good with the other, lifted a finger to Harley, "My father said there wasn't enough gas in that truck to get very far and he wanted to go after Eileen on foot. I told him we should wait. We would have to carry a can of gas with us if we didn't want to walk back up here pushing the truck."

The old man frowned. "That gas gauge don't work no more; it's stuck on one-quarter tank. I keep extra gasoline in cans in the brush arbor. You know…people who live so far from town have to be careful." He scowled even darker this time. "I carry a five-gallon gas can in the back of that truck, too, but I let a man at the sing have it." He thought back to the encounter. "The crazy old man knew he didn't have enough gas to get back home, even before he left. He figured someone would have a little extra though, and no one would be so rude as to refuse an old man enough gasoline to get back home on."

Willie pulled a face at this. "So, you gave him the last of your gasoline?"

Willie's father shook his head at his bad luck, "I was the first one he asked. I knew, then, it would be nip and tuck getting home all right, but I had to let him have it. People would have thought ill of me if I hadn't." He grimaced in the direction of the sing which lay many roundabout miles to the northeast—though not so far as the crow flies. "There was a woman there who I think had her eye on me, and you know how women always like a generous man." He was getting riled again as he recalled the woman at the sing. "She later suggested she might need a ride home, but I had to tell her I didn't have enough gasoline left. She wasn't so pleased with me then I can tell you. I was damn lucky to make it back home myself." He looked toward the summer hogan. "I meant to fill up the tank today…if I'd got the chance. Good thing I didn't though, I guess; that truck might be clear out of the country by now."

Willie attempted to further calm her old father by suggesting, "Eileen maybe just got nervous waiting here—she's not used to being so far away from town." Aunt Willie turned to Harley Ponyboy. "After you left, Eileen seemed to calm down a little and I thought she might be okay with being out here. But I should have seen, after Elma left, that I was wrong about that."

Harley shook his head and sighed, "Well it wasn't your fault, Auntie, but now I got ta go find her before something happens to her."

The old man threw a hand in the direction of the highway and gave his final opinion on the matter, "I think that little woman can take care of herself all right."

Harley frowned at this but didn't answer. He was well aware Eileen could take care of herself, but was afraid now what direction that might take.

When the old man went to fetch his remaining gas can from the arbor, Harley took the opportunity to ask his aunt if she still had the old Long Colt revolver, telling her, "I loaned my shotgun to that T'sí boy who lives down second canyon. His grandparents have gone off and left him. He needed a gun for the coyotes."

Willie looked askance at her nephew. "I know those people...they wouldn't leave that boy alone...not without a very good reason."

Harley only shrugged and then, when she still didn't go for the gun, he gestured toward the hogan.

His aunt nodded, "I'll get the Long Colt."

Harley stood watching as the sunset left patches of fire splashed along the canyon rim. He was wondering if Eileen was seeing the sunset, too, and if she was thinking of him as she did...probably not.

When his Aunt Willie reappeared, her eyes were as empty as her hands and she looked down the road to spit in disgust.

"She has the Long Colt," she murmured.

Harley looked in the same direction and nodded but said nothing, only went to help the old man with the gas cans.

On the ride to retrieve the stranded truck, neither Harley nor his aunt said anything to the old man about the pistol being gone. They didn't want to get him started again.

Harley hooked his chain to their truck and pulled it out of the ditch with a jerk. The old man, being careful not to spill a single drop, poured in his can of gasoline. Willie cranked the engine, five or ten seconds at a time, but it was nearly a minute before enough gas reached the carburetor to cause the engine to start. There was a clatter of valves as it spit carbon and disgorged smoke until the ground was covered in a fine fog.

Willie was now determined to follow Harley back down country to see how the boy, Arnold T'sí, was doing, and if his people had returned. If not, she meant to stay with him till she saw what was what.

Grover pointed to the left front wheel of the truck. "That wheel might be bent; it was wobbling when Harley pulled it out. If we are lucky it's *only* the wheel, and not something worse." He stared at the offending part with an eye born of long experience driving in rough country. "We better just get it home where I got some tools; there's no use in making things worse than they already are." Dusk had fallen while they talked, making the old man anxious to get the truck home before full dark.

Aunt Willie, still speaking in Navajo, nodded her head at her father. "No, you are right…take the truck home. I will go with Harley—he can drop me off at the T'sí place." Her chin was set, and when her father saw that he knew arguing would do no good. He turned to go but his daughter hadn't finished.

"If you can fix the truck you can pick me up tomorrow," she called after him. Then added hopefully, "Maybe you'll only have to put on the spare wheel." She then glanced over at Harley. "I'm not leaving that boy down there alone tonight, not with all these goings on."

15

The Nighthawk

Claude Bell sat at the wheel of a nearly new pickup truck—stolen, early that same night, from the parking lot of the Thunderbird Motel in Farmington. It was his second score in two days. He had always been good at stealing cars, and this base model Ford took only a few moments. He felt the secret to success in this sort of endeavor was in not keeping the vehicle any longer than absolutely necessary.

"Choose your target with a specific purpose in mind—then abandon the unit as fast and inconspicuously as possible." He'd learned that in prison...and a good many other things too. Prison had proven to be more of a government finishing school for those young street toughs who were of a mind to finish their education in crime. To his way of thinking, this was a major point separating a person who knew his business from one who didn't. He had been arrested a number of times over the years, and for a variety of crimes, but never had he been arrested for stealing a car. He felt there was a good chance this latest acquisition would not even be reported until morning. He had only one stop left to make, and that was at the liquor store at the edge of town.

Eileen had been harder to keep up with than he first imagined. But then, he had known from the start, she was a cut above most when it came to smart. They were much the same in that regard and he thought that might have been what attracted him to her in the first place. He knew a lot about Eileen—gleaned in bits and pieces during their stay at the Bible Center. He'd had great hopes for the two of them, thinking it might well be the fresh start both so badly needed. The team leader breaking in on them like that—well, that was the man's own bad luck: it surprised Claude…set off that little thing in his head; he still wasn't sure what happened after that.

Claude was not so naive as to think there was still a chance of he and Eileen getting back together. No, that wouldn't be happening now. Now, there was nothing for it but to make sure she didn't talk, and there was only one sure way to prevent that.

The very idea of this blanket-head, Harley Ponyboy, having the effrontery to assume her protection, raised his ire. If the man's friend, Alfred Nakii, was any indicator of the caliber of people Eileen had taken up with, this Harley Ponyboy should not be much of a problem. The first thing, of course, was to locate the pair. Alfred, when pressed, had made the place they were headed sound more like a small community rather than the sparsely populated wild side of hell that it actually turned out to be.

It had taken Claude only a few hours to realize it could take weeks to find the pair. Unfortunately, he didn't have that kind of time.

What few people he'd run across, those who would even talk to him, were standoffish, suspicious, and not inclined to be at all friendly. He would have thought he appeared Indian enough to generate some sort of rapport, but there was something else causing them to disconnect when questioned about Eileen. Even the young man he gave a lift to, and shared a good bit of whiskey with, had left him with the impression he knew more than he was willing to say. Claude left the young man at the next dirt crossroads, obviously feeling the effects of the alcohol. The youth, clearly educated beyond the norm, refused to have anymore to drink, saying his brother would be along for him most any time and would tell their parents if he suspected there'd been drinking. The last thing he offered was, "If I were you, *Hastiin*, I would be very careful about asking after this woman you're looking for. This is a different part of the reservation than you might be used to; there is the chance she is better left unfound." Claude thought this odd, but was not a man easily discouraged when the stakes were high.

He barely had time to reach fourth gear on his way back to the highway, when in the distance, he saw a middle-aged woman crossing the road ahead of a rather large flock of sheep, who in turn, were being nipped along by two dogs. Hearing his truck, the woman turned in the middle of the highway and waved her arms, then turned her hands palm down and patted the air as a signal for him to slow down. Claude let the truck drift to a stop alongside, smiled at the woman, and attempted to engage her in conversation. He was not unskilled at this—it was the rare woman he couldn't charm into some sort of banter. When this particular woman appeared uninterested, however, he was forced to come right out with it; asking if she had seen a stranger...a woman...new to the area. The woman was his sister, he said, and he had been told she'd moved up this way with her new husband: a man called Harley Ponyboy. He then went on to describe Eileen—being sure to mention she might not look quite the same now. The older woman cocked her head to one side and paid close attention to all he said, but when he was finished she looked him up and down with a flinty eye. "You say she might have red hair...or she might have black hair...and it might be long...or it might be cut short?" She shook her head, and without waiting for him to answer she turned to her sheep. "This woman you're looking for could be anyone. A man should keep in closer touch with his sister, I think."

Claude watched the woman for a moment as she directed her dogs in gathering the now scattered band of sheep; a deadly calm fell over him...just as it always did when that little thing in his head clicked into place. He made his way back to the pull-off, the one just across Highway 163, where he parked well off the pavement, concealed by a county road grader and a giant culvert that had lain there over a month waiting to be installed. He had a clear view of the highway in both directions...and of anyone coming to or from that country to the west.

The soft call of a night bird drifted through his partially lowered window. Claude couldn't recall its Indian name and had never heard what it was called in English. His own people thought them an omen—of what, he couldn't remember.

This waiting game was a long shot and he knew it. Some of the people living out here might go into town only once a month, a few even less. He did, at least, know what Harley Ponyboy's pickup looked like; Alfred Nakii had described it in great detail. The man had just been stalling for time, of course. It was toward the end—when Alfred would have said anything to escape the pain.

Claude had picked up a bag of chips at the liquor store in town and a clutch of bottles filled with what advertised itself as 'crystal spring water.' There were also a few sticks of dry sausage that left his teeth with a greasy orange film and a lingering taste of stale garlic. Not a supper he could recommend, but he was a man used to simple fare and had known worse.

It was nearly dark, and vehicles already had their lights on, as they sped along the two-lane asphalt ribbon. None slowed, or turned west at the crossing, and each loud passing left a mind-numbing silence in its wake. Twenty minutes later, Claude noticed two faint pinpricks of light far across the highway and to the west...unmistakably a vehicle...though still a good distance off. Occasionally obscured by wind-blown dust, or a dip in the gravel road, he still was certain it was a pickup truck. As it came nearer it slowed to a stop just across from the pull-off. When finally the passenger door opened and the overhead light came on, Claude could make out three people in the cab. He thought two of the people were adults; the third appeared to be a smaller person, a child possibly. This caused him to come instantly alert and concentrate every sense in that direction. It was the smallest of the three who eventually stepped down from the truck, and Claude could see she carried a small bag in one hand. It was a woman, he thought. She reached into the bag and handed someone inside the truck something, then waved as she watched the driver turn the truck around and drive off into the gathering gloom.

Claude waited until the truck nearly disappeared in the distance—still not willing to believe his luck. He felt there was a good chance it was Eileen. He saw her stand for a moment, shoulders seeming to slump, as she followed the dusty retreat of the old pickup. When she turned back to the highway, it was to cross over to his side of the pavement, where she barely even glanced about, before taking up the familiar stance of a hitchhiker. Only when the next car flashed by could Claude satisfy himself it was really her. He slid down in the seat—just peeping over the dashboard—confident he'd gone unnoticed. It was a rare woman that would have the courage to hitchhike that lonely stretch at night…that…or a very desperate one. The wind was on the rise, and as it would with a deer or an elk, it seemed to make her nervous; she shrugged occasionally inside her light jacket, and fidgeted with her bag, as she looked up and down the highway.

She obviously intended to hitch north in the direction of Salt Lake City, probably still determined to be with her relatives. Her back was to him and she seemed unaware of his dark colored truck, invisible there in the shadows of the oversize culvert. He would have to handle this very carefully. Turning on his lights, or starting the engine, would probably frighten her—not a good thing—as he knew, for a fact, Eileen was the type to break and run should she be given half a chance. Fortunately, there was not much in the way of cover for a good distance in any direction. He might just have to risk it—try to run her down—before some soft-hearted or lecherous person came along and offered her a ride. It was now quite dark; he could barely make out the woman's outline as she stood waiting there at the edge of the deserted highway.

The wind, when it came, blew from several directions before clocking from the northwest and blowing harder, with gusts well beyond its first promise. The slight figure by the highway turned her back to the sting of driven sand and shrugged deep into her light jacket. Earlier in the day, and far to the north of Hanksville, a frontal system was making up along the rocky spine that marks the domed escarpment of Capital Reef. It looked for a while like it might hang up on the snowy peaks of the Manti-LaSalles but then fooled forecasters by breaking away to the south, only to be baffled by the Goose Necks of the San Juan. Tearing loose in a rage the rogue front sent gales twisting and writhing their way down Glen Canyon, where they picked up speed across the open reaches of Lake Powell. By the time the winds sifted through the flats below Mexican Hat, the air was filled with a choking red dust—piling up sand against the scattered hogans of the *Diné* in that lonely land. People reported the backhanded slap of the storm as far away as Many Farms and Chinle.

~~~~~~

A short string of cars appeared coming from the north—tourists, likely, out of Moab—heading home after a few days among the four-wheeling and bike trails the area is famous for. They seemed in a hurry now to return to their workaday lives; too short a respite, and one that brought people to the limit of their endurance yet, strangely, refreshed them in mind and spirit. They felt gritty and longed for a hot shower…and food without sand in it. Not one of them noticed the hitchhiker huddled at the far roadside. They remained oblivious to the drama playing out on this darkened stretch of 163.

He would wait for these last few vehicles to get past then take a run at her. There was really no escaping him this time. Thinking ahead, Claude concluded he might, himself, continue on to Moab—pick up a new ride—one that might carry him on to Denver and old friends. Maybe he could find some sort of sanctuary there. He still had plenty of the old Navajo's money left…money that might yet buy a new truck…but not for foolish old Benny Klee.

The gusting winds drove curtains of sand—at times obscuring everything beyond a few yards. Each time Claude lost view of the slight figure at the roadside he became anxious, and finally, muffled by a mounting gale, he started the engine and made ready. Having memorized every dip and gravel rut between him and his target he would need the headlights only in the final moments—at which point there would be little possibility of escape.

Just as he put the truck in gear, however, there came yet another dim glow of headlights—approaching from the south this time. He reconsidered as he lightly touched the brake pedal, giving no thought to the truck's taillights, which momentarily flashed red against the culvert. He caught this little indiscretion in the side mirror, causing him to curse and ease the truck out of gear. He watched as the oncoming headlights grew stronger, then gnashed his teeth as the vehicle rolled to a stop beside the hitch-hiker. Just for a fleeting instant, he saw the woman glance his way as the door opened and someone pulled her inside.

~~~~~~

Thomas Begay saw fear on the woman's face and quickly yanked her in beside him, then motioned Charlie Yazzie to gun the truck. With tires squealing, the vehicle veered left across the highway and up the road leading into the backcountry. In the rear view mirror Charlie saw a set of headlights switch on, but only for a moment, as though to have a better look at their vehicle as it sped away. The person didn't follow, as far as Thomas could see, and when he looked again there were no lights or sign of pursuit.

Neither Thomas nor Charlie said a word—nor did Eileen May—as she clutched her bag, sat bolt upright, and stared straight ahead. She had immediately recognized the Tribal emblem on the truck door, and thinking it the lesser of two evils, instantly made her choice. She'd sensed someone watching her from the darkness—long before the brake lights came on—

and even thought she'd caught a reflective glint from the headlights of a passing car. She tried to tell herself it was from the road equipment parked near the culvert but the fear was on her then, and she recalled Harley Ponyboy's last words to her: "Eileen, you can only be safe here at Aunt Willie's. You don't know what might be waiting for you out there. Stay here and I will come for you. You'll be safer here than anywhere else." They proved to be wise words. Still, when she listened from inside the hogan as Willie's friend told of the stranger and his questions, a cold sweat came over her and she was certain it would be only a matter of time before Claude Bell discovered her hiding place.

Thomas was the first to speak and tried sounding casual, "You must be Harley's new friend?"

Eileen pursed her lips slightly, turned to look at him, and only then recognized him as the person who came to the trailer to check on Harley. She nodded, and nodded again at Charlie. "And you two must be Harley's friends, Charlie Yazzie and Thomas Begay?" She turned back to her side window peering out into the dark, before saying, "Harley talks a lot about you two." She seemed to relax a little, "I guess you showed up just in time. I've got a pretty good idea who that was back there."

"So do we." Charlie didn't turn to look at her and was already fumbling with his microphone. He soon had Tribal Officer Billy Red Clay on the radio, and though the reception was poor, the investigator knew it would get worse the farther they went into the canyon. He made it clear to Billy they had Eileen May with them and said he felt certain Claude Bell was in close proximity—possibly even following them. He went on to say they were en route to Aunt Willie Etcitty's camp—where they hoped to find Harley before he ran up against this man suspected in the killing of Benny Klee, Alfred Nakii, and possibly even Gilbert Nez. Charlie gave their location twice and hoped the increasing static didn't prevent it being heard.

Billy Red Clay after several attempts, finally acknowledged the transmission and assured them the FBI, in conjunction with Utah and New Mexico state troopers, would have roadblocks set up on 163 in both directions. "Claude Bell isn't familiar with this country and I doubt he can work his way out of the area without hitting one or the other of those check-points." Nothing further was heard for nearly a full minute. Billy then surprised them by coming back on. "I'm on my way, Charlie, and Agent Smith is right behind me. Fred intends to stop this guy, one way or the other, but wants you people up there to avoid in-teracting with him…and hopefully keep the woman out of harm's way until we get there. Eileen May's testimony could be crucial in this case." This mes-sage came in very clear despite local two-way interference from the gathering of the various agen-cies.

Thomas smiled at this and shook his head at Charlie, knowing full well there was little chance they were going to stand down and wait for the FBI to get there. *No…that probably wouldn't happen.* He whispered for Charlie to ask his nephew how he pro-posed they should go about staying away from this killer should he already be on their tail.

Charlie grinned and passed along the question.

There was a pause. Then Agent Fred Smith came on, asking, "Charlie, are you armed?"

"Roger that Fred, I am armed. We're not sure if Bell is though. We'll do our best to stay ahead of him...assuming he's even following us."

There was a crackle of static and Charlie thought he heard Billy Red Clay say something about his position. That was followed by Fred Smith, who only by chance, came in clean and clear and again impressed upon them the importance of not engaging the suspect in any sort of confrontation. "Assume the suspect is armed and just try to stay out of his way until we arrive, Charlie." A long string of static and garbled interference put an end to the conversation. They were fast running out of range.

16

Friends

It was already dark by the time Harley Ponyboy pulled away from Arnold T'si's grandparent's place. His Aunt Willie had immediately taken charge of the boy and made herself busy putting together something for him to eat. She tried to get Harley to stay long enough to have something, but he was in no frame of mind to linger. Eileen could be in trouble even as he stood there, and he'd never forgive himself, he declared, should anything happen to her.

Aunt Willie pouted, but could guess the things going through her nephew's mind, and grudgingly agreed. She tossed him two apples that were in a bowl on the table. Harley put them in his jacket pocket along with the handful of shotgun shells the boy had returned. He picked up his old shotgun and nodded to Arnold, who didn't smile but gave a little wave of his hand.

Considering the state of the road and weather, Harley felt he might be pushing his old truck beyond reason. Going this fast was foolish and only invited more trouble. Even so, he'd made no more than a half-dozen miles before a set of headlights popped up over a rise. Harley, thinking it might at last be Charlie and Thomas, flashed his lights and pulled to the side of the road. He soon saw it wasn't his friends at all but rather the missing grandparents of Arnold T'si—safe and hurrying home to their grandson.

The old woman peered cautiously through the glass thinking they'd had enough excitement for one day, and enough of strangers in a country not usually prone to them. Still, when the man made that little circular motion with his finger asking her to roll down her window it would have been rude of her not to comply.

Harley introduced himself to the old couple, told them he had spoken to their grandson earlier, and that his Aunt Willie was there now with Arnold. The old woman had known Willie Etcitty for years and was visibly relieved to hear the woman was now with her grandson.

The woman was quick to say they would not ordinarily have left Arnold alone, but he was not yet back with the sheep when a woman had come to their camp and insisted they give her a ride to the highway. She told them her truck had broken down leaving her stranded. The woman was clearly distraught— promising them a good bit of money just to take her down to the highway. She said it was important she get to town. There was a desperate look about her— they thought—and when she opened her bag to prove she had money they couldn't help but see the revolver in there with it. At this point they felt it prudent not to argue. It was plain the woman was determined and they could only believe she intended to accomplish her agenda—one way or the other. When they finally

177

agreed to take her, the old man insisted he go along rather than wait there for their grandson to bring in the sheep. He couldn't drive anymore, he said, but it was an old truck and broke down a lot. He might be able to fix it should something go wrong. His wife looked sideways at him and knew it was not the truck he was worried about.

When Harley questioned the old couple further, she admitted, yes, they had, in fact, just taken the woman down to the crossroads where she told them she would catch a ride. The old couple advised it might be dangerous for a lone woman on that stretch of road so late in the evening, but she had only laughed and patted her bag, saying she carried a great magic to ward off such evil.

The old man, finally anxious to be off, leaned across his wife and thanked Harley again for helping with their grandson and assured him he would be welcome at their place anytime. He turned then to his wife and whispered they must be on their way. The couple bid Harley goodbye and then rolling up the window, hurried off.

Harley sat a moment listening to blowing sand pepper the side of the truck, wondering what Eileen's plan might have been? Was she going to wait for him by the highway until he happened to return? Or did she have something else in mind—something that didn't include him? He put the truck in gear with only two things clear in his mind. He must first find out if Eileen was safe, and barring that, he must somehow hook up with Thomas and Charlie who might know better how to proceed.

Harley was still some miles from the junction with 163 when the storm began to abate—a light rain leaving a layer of murky silt on the windshield. *Only enough rain to turn dust to mud,* he thought.

The windshield wipers didn't work. They were on his list, at home, under: "needed truck repairs." Thomas had made the list for him soon after Harley bought the vehicle. So far, the only work he'd accomplished was the installation of a fancy shift knob found on sale at the Co-op, and a bumper sticker that read, "I survived boarding school." It hadn't been easy finding that sticker, but he felt it made an important social statement. He'd had one just like it on his last truck and people seemed to relate to it...pointing and waving from time to time. Neither item was on Thomas's list—leaving a good many things still to be done.

Harley could now only hope he would hit another little shower, one strong enough to wash away the mud and allow a little better visibility. Actually stopping the truck to get out and wipe off the windshield by hand never occurred to him, nor would it to most men.

17

The Fox

By the time Thomas Begay and Charlie Yazzie drew out the greater part of Eileen's story, they were thinking the woman might be more victim than anything— caught up in something not of her own making, while pursuing an honest turnaround in her life. Her recent actions now appeared to be a course any person might have followed in similar circumstances. They could see, now, how their friend Harley Ponyboy was so taken by this attractive and plain-spoken woman. She had a sense about her that led them to believe she was indeed what she purported to be.

Once the winds died, and fast moving rain showers tapered off, a full moon rose plump and golden above the mesas. Thomas took this as a good omen. Charlie partially agreed; not so much that it was an omen, but that it might now be possible to drive without lights for a while. Though this might slow them down a bit, he reckoned it to be worth the lost time. It might even allow them an opportunity to detect their pursuer...should there actually be a pursuer. The moon alone now provided enough light for Charlie to maintain a reasonable pace. He geared the truck down as needed, avoiding the use of taillights which might mark their location and possibly give them away. Thomas watched this maneuver with satisfaction guessing his friend had learned something from him after all. Thomas had often used that ploy in the past and now was pleased to see Charlie taking advantage of that knowledge. So far, Thomas hadn't seen any indication of headlights from behind, or for that matter, any telltale sign at all that someone might be following. Thomas Begay was not one to mince words; so when he finally turned to Eileen it was to ask her, straight up, where she thought her relationship with Harley Ponyboy might be going. "Harley's an old friend of ours and we would hate to see him get hurt...he already has enough trouble in his life as it is."

Eileen shot him a sharp glance and was quick to reply, "Not that it's anyone's business...but truth is...we haven't had time to develop much of a relationship." Here Eileen leveled a calculating gaze at the two. "I'll be sure to let you guys know what's between us...once we figure it out ourselves."

Thomas sat back, gazing out into the night with a blank look on his face. "Fair enough, Eileen."

Charlie knew Thomas wasn't used to being confronted in so forthright a manner. He estimated the woman's stock had gone up several points.

It was another several minutes before Thomas ventured another question. "What's in the bag, Eileen?"

She didn't turn or look. "Just some clean underwear, a Bible...and a gun."

Both men chuckled at this. The woman had a sense of humor. This was another plus as far as they were concerned.

Thomas was first to notice vehicle lights approaching from the higher terrain to the west but thought them still a good way off. Charlie indicated, with a nod, that he also saw the lights, and then with a shove of his chin at the glove box, signaled Thomas to pull out the .38.

"Make sure that's loaded, will you." Charlie thought it time they were prepared for even the most unlikely eventuality.

One of the bright spots of Thomas Begay's life was to be in charge of the Chief's Special: Charlie's snub-nosed Smith & Wesson. Thomas often termed it their 'good luck piece' as he thought it had averted several runs of bad luck over the years.

As he slowed the truck and began looking for a place to pull over, Charlie knew it wasn't Claude Bell or Billy Red Clay coming their way; as those two should both still be somewhere behind them. He sincerely hoped Billy would catch up to the fugitive before innocent people came to harm. He was fairly certain he and Thomas could handle the suspect, should it come to that, but there was Eileen to consider now. Harley Ponyboy also remained an unknown in the equation, though Charlie was certain his friend was desperately searching for Eileen.

At this time of night there was little reason for traffic on these isolated roads, making it even more likely the approaching headlights would be Harley Ponyboy. It would be just like Harley to pop up when least expected. The little man now seemed past all reason and subject to go blindly off in any direction. All this was working on Charlie's mind as they sat waiting at the edge of the dirt road—their own lights dowsed and Thomas Begay trying to load the .38 in the dark. Several scenarios crossed his mind in regard to what might lie ahead; none were reassuring.

The three people in the truck watched apprehensively as the approaching vehicle slowed; the other driver obviously now aware of them...but cautious... unsure who *they* might be.

Peering into the glare of the lights, Charlie momentarily glanced across Eileen to see how Thomas was coming with the revolver.

"Let me have it," he said finally and reached for the gun.

Thomas snapped shut the fully loaded cylinder— frowned in the dark—but passed him the revolver. He understood the investigator would be leery of someone firing across him in the event a quick shot should be required.

Harley was already grinning ear to ear as he pulled abreast and saw the three of them together— Eileen apparently unharmed. He rolled down his window to reveal the barrel of his shotgun leaned carelessly across the window frame. A trickle of mud dribbled off the roof of the truck and a bit fell on his nose causing him to look up and move the gun to the seat. His wave was directed past the two men obviously targeting Eileen; he looked relieved as she waved back with a wan little smile.

Ignoring his friends, Harley saw only Eileen. He hesitated to speak—not daring to ask if she was all right but at the same time wanting her to know all was forgiven. Finally, unable to contain himself, he just burst out with it, "Eileen, are you okay? Aunt Willie and I have been worried sick something might have happened ta you!"

Eileen smiled at this. "Something did almost happen to me, Harley, but thanks to these two, it didn't."

Harley reveled in the sound of her voice without any real grasp of what she said. He focused instead on her teeth, remarkably white in the darkened truck. Her reply had fairly flown past him. "So, you're okay?"

"I'm just fine Harley." Apologies didn't come easy for Eileen. "Sorry for the worry—I'm not sure what came over me—taking off like that, I mean. Just scared I guess."

"Well, the main thing is, you're all right now Eileen." Harley smiled happily at her while still ignoring the other two, causing them to glance sideways at one another and lean even further back out of the line of conversation.

Thomas, becoming impatient and unable to hold back any longer, frowned and held up a hand. "Excuse me, folks, but we may have another visitor along here any minute now and that could be either good or bad depending on who might get here first."

Charlie nodded his affirmation of Thomas's concern.

Harley snorted, "So, Claude is already out here somewhere?" He slowly shook his head and sounded weary then muttered, "I been afraid of that." Harley, still not inquiring how Eileen wound up with the pair, guessed another encounter with Claude Bell was probably imminent.

Thomas Begay confirmed this. "That character may be somewhere behind us even though we haven't seen any actual sign of him so far. He could be running with his lights off...like we were until you came along."

Harley immediately reached down and turned off his own lights, then cautiously searched the dark, though there was now even less to see.

Charlie finished the update by saying, "Billy Red Clay and FBI Agent Smith are somewhere between Farmington and here. They should be getting close about now. Smith is bound and determined to take Bell in, no matter what. He wants us to lay low and avoid any contact if possible."

Charlie had only the glimmer of a plan. "Agent Smith has requested road blocks in both directions on 163 but we're pretty sure now the guy is already sandwiched in between Billy and us. We don't think Bell's armed, but Benny Klee's wife mentioned her husband owned a pistol and might have had it in the truck with him the morning he was killed. Authorities didn't find a gun—but that doesn't mean there wasn't one—and Claude Bell might have it now."

Thomas seemed ambivalent. "I don't care whether he has a gun or not. This guy owes us for Alfred Nakii." Here Thomas's voice fell, "...and maybe for Gilbert Nez, too. My father wasn't much, I guess, but he shouldn't have ended up like he did."

"Be that as it may," and Charlie was now clearly adamant in this regard, "we need to take this one step at a time. No flying off the handle!" Thomas was famous for flying off the handle, and his friends had seen ample evidence of it over the years; it almost always left a mess. "I think we should head on up to Willie Etcitty's place and get ready... in case Bell finds us. If he shows...fine...we'll do what we have to do, regardless of what Billy Red Clay or Agent Smith thinks proper." This suited Thomas, and Harley Ponyboy was quick to nod agreement as well. Eileen, for her part, remained silent and offered no hint of what she was thinking.

"Eileen, do you want to ride with me on the way up to Aunt Willie's?" Harley, hesitant to ask to begin with, instantly regretted it when she sighed, shaking her head.

"No, Harley. I'm fine right here. Besides...you know that passenger door pops open when you hit a bump." That wasn't the real reason, of course, and everyone knew it.

Harley looked over at the door in question and nodded; it was, indeed, already ajar. He frowned and reached across the seat to re-shut it. He looked lost for a moment as he watched Eileen change places with Thomas. She didn't look at him again.

~~~~~~

Grover Etcitty was asleep in the brush arbor as the little entourage pulled up to Willie's hogan. The noise and truck lights didn't wake the old man and everyone was pleased about that.

Eileen went inside with Harley's aunt; the two apparently making their peace as they began fixing coffee and rustling up food.

Harley sacked out in the bed of his truck with the tailgate down—his old shotgun beside him and the handful of shells close to hand. He'd been on a dead run for two days and was having a hard time keeping his eyes open, despite his continuing worry over Eileen.

The other two sat on the tailgate of Charlie's pickup and talked quietly as they watched down the canyon. The last mile or so into camp was steep and rough—they doubted anyone could drive in at night without lights. The canyon walls were already beginning to block the last of the moon as it continued to slide below the rim. Neither of the men appeared tired despite a rather full day of their own. They could see a good distance down the road, and relied on Willie's dog to warn of any approach from the outlying scatter of trees. The dog had taken to them at once, only requiring Willie to speak harshly in Navajo the one time, and that, even before they got down from the truck.

Willie Etcitty brought coffee, which Thomas and Charlie were happy to have. Harley, when she asked, declined, saying he'd best catch a few winks first. His aunt came closer and asked if there was something else she might get him. Then, dropping her voice to a whisper, confided to her nephew that Eileen had returned the old Long Colt, saying she hadn't meant to hurt anyone with it; she just didn't want Grover shooting at her if he caught her hijacking the truck. Willie talked quietly to her nephew for a few minutes before leaving a sack of sandwiches and a folded blanket on the tailgate. Just as she turned to go she gave the blanket a knowing look and then nodded at her nephew.

Charlie, still sitting and sipping his coffee, barely closed his eyes when Thomas nudged him back awake. It took the investigator only an instant to come aware but when he reached his hand for the revolver, it was gone. Thomas was already slipping off the tailgate to stand gazing into the foggy dawn... watching as headlights snaked up the road...close enough now to hear tires feeling their way up the rocky track. When the vehicle high-centered on a sandstone slab, the engine snarled and a muffled clash of gears caused tires to squeal, then grab, with the screech of metal across sandstone. It took only a few moments more for the police unit to materialize––louder now without its muffler. Thomas had moved only a step or so from the truck, the .38 held loosely at his side. He gave Charlie Yazzie an almost imperceptible shake of his head, then turned to hand him back the revolver.

"It's my nephew and it sounds like he may be needing a mechanic."

Charlie looked over at Harley Ponyboy and saw him lowering the barrel of the shotgun, laying it aside as he rolled off the back of his pickup. Charlie kept his seat—put the .38 in his jacket pocket—and then sat silent...waiting.

Billy Red Clay eased up into the yard and nonchalantly got down from his unit then moved off into the trees where he took a leak. He returned, zipping his pants, and his eyes played across the other three men in the clearing. "Where's the woman?"

Harley came forward, pulling on his jacket, and rubbing sleep from his eyes. "Eileen's inside with my Aunt Willie...probably asleep."

The other two moved closer to the Tribal policeman—Charlie looking anxiously back down the road. "Fred Smith didn't follow you up here?"

"No, he didn't. He stayed down below to coordinate the search and roadblocks. He had the state police set up a command post across from the cutoff." Billy pushed back his hat and scratched his forehead. "They don't see much chance of Bell making it out of the area and Fred said he wanted to be there when they got him." The policeman sounded serious, "I just wanted to make sure he hadn't already slipped past us...maybe even be lurking around up here somewhere." Billy scanned the canyon rim as he spoke. "Agent Smith caught me on the radio about an hour ago...another mile or two and I'd a been out of range."

Charlie nodded as though he understood what Thomas's nephew was talking about. "The thought crossed our mind he might have gotten around us, but we were ready for him."

Billy Red Clay shook out a set of handcuffs and moved toward the hogan. "You better go get her now, Harley. I'm going to have to take her in."

"Whoa!" In two steps Thomas was between Harley and his nephew, one hand already holding the little man back.

Harley could barely speak. "You don't mean to cuff her and haul her off...do you Billy?" he looked confused but there was something else there too. "Where are you taking her?"

Thomas knew instantly his friend was on the verge of an irretrievable decision—and one that might have far-reaching consequences. He had seen that look before and knew Harley's next move might be a violent one. The two of them had been through a lot over the years and while Harley was probably the least excitable person he knew, even *he* was capable of reacting with reckless abandon should a situation turn desperate.

Charlie also looked startled at the policeman's actions. "I don't see any need for that, Billy. We're just talking protective custody here, right?" Charlie edged up and laid yet another restraining hand on Harley Ponyboy's shoulder. He, too, knew the signs.

Billy Red Clay shook his head at the others. "I'm sorry boys...things have changed since we talked last night." His tone was apologetic, but firm. "When Fred Smith hooked up with the state boys down there, they had a message for him to call his office in Farmington. Apparently they hadn't been able to reach him on the radio." Billy chose his words carefully now. "It seems their lab people in Albuquerque may have identified several of those sketchy prints left in Benny Klee's pickup. They were wiped down like the rest...but a few left slight acidic etchings...not really enough to get a fix on as yet, but they're working on it." Billy took a deep breath and watched Harley from the corner of his eye. "Forensics was able to rebuild several of those prints based on fresher ones lifted from Harley's trailer; their people made a pass through there when they were investigating the Alfred Nakii homicide. They think they may be able to tie prints found there to those in the pickup." Billy looked directly at Harley and it was clear he hated what came next. "Harley, that might mean Eileen May was in that truck when Benny Klee was killed."

The wind seemed to go out of Harley Ponyboy, leaving him physically weak and speechless. Charlie exchanged glances with Thomas as the tall *Diné* led Harley to his truck and sat him back down on the tailgate. Harley was stronger than most people could imagine and Thomas Begay didn't intend letting his friend attempt some last minute effort to help Eileen––at least, not if he could help it, he wouldn't.

Charlie and Billy Red Clay turned back to the hogan. The investigator, seeing Billy un-holster his sidearm, followed suit...more of a reflex action than anything else. Who either of them might be required to shoot remained unclear, even to them.

Just as the policeman approached the door and reached out to knock, it burst open to reveal Willie Etcitty Eileen's right arm wrapped around her neck and a gun stuck in Willie's ribs. For Charlie, the scene was so bizarre as to instantly cause a freeze-frame in his mind's eye. The pistol, a mean looking little automatic, was at full cock—a Walther .380 possibly—a weapon designed for close-up killing. It would make a big entry...deadly at close range.

Eileen was dressed in worn pants and a shirt given her by Willie Etcitty. The two women were of a size and even the old boots fit her well. "Charlie...you and the cop can drop those guns and kick them over this way." Eileen's voice was calm, almost friendly, as she reassured them. "No one has to die

191

here today guys." She jammed the pistol's muzzle under Willie's chin, causing the older woman to tilt her head back slightly, making her appear even more vulnerable. "Willie and I are just going for a little ride...that's all." Then she further emphasized, "No one's going to get hurt, if you listen very carefully, and do exactly as I say...DROP THE GUNS!" Eileen's tone left no room for hesitation or negotiation. Both men tossed down their weapons.

Harley saw his Aunt Willie flinch, though she showed no sign of fear. She appeared almost as calm as her captor, nearly to the point of indifference from what he could see. He wondered how long Eileen had been listening to them. The two women...the most important women left in his life... stood balanced on the verge of a potentially lethal tragedy. One or the other...maybe both...might soon be dead. As short as their relationship had been, it was clear to Harley that Eileen meant what she said and probably wouldn't hesitate to act should her hand be forced. It was obvious she was struggling under an increasingly dark veil of hopelessness, possibly the most dangerous emotion to affect the human spirit.

"Eileen, how about you trade Willie for me?" Harley spoke impulsively, without considering the consequences. "You're going to need a good driver and you can't drive and keep an eye on Willie at the same time. I grew up in this country. I know it as well as anyone, and if anyone can get you out of here it would be me." Harley's mind came alive—his aunt's welfare now his first priority. Almost as strong was his belief that Eileen could not have been any part of what Billy Red Clay was alleging. *She was not that kind of person. No, that was impossible.* "What do you say, Eileen? You can keep that pistol on me...I doubt you could shoot *me* anyway."

"Really Harley? Really! You think I won't shoot you? That's a big bet little man..." Eileen touched the tip of her tongue to her teeth indicating she might be giving the idea serious thought.

Harley, not relaxing his position, spoke again and in a tone that left no doubt. "It's no gamble for me, Eileen. I probably don't have any future without you anyway, but together...we just might have a shot."

Charlie looked across at Thomas and warily shook his head in warning. Then he glanced at Billy Red Clay, who in turn sighed and nodded silently, conceding they no longer held any cards.

Poor Willie Etcitty didn't change expression or give any indication what she might be thinking.

Eileen pondered Harley Ponyboy's offer, and in less time than it takes to tell, made her decision. While she was convinced there was little chance of a happy outcome, she did think her chances with Harley to be better than with his aunt. She considered herself without any other viable alternative. At this point she could only put one foot in front of the other and hope for a bit of luck. She'd known for a while now such a time would be coming, but had pretty much refused to think beyond the present.

"Thomas, you let Harley go." Eileen's voice carried the deadly certainty of last resort. When he hesitated, Eileen's eyes narrowed to mere slits. "I mean right now!"

"Now wait a minute..." Before Thomas could finish, a bullet from Eileen's pistol smacked through the fender and only inches from his hand. Thomas looked at the hole and then at Eileen and was certain she hadn't the slightest idea where that bullet was going to hit. She knew when she fired it she might kill him.

Charlie didn't take his eyes off her and his determination was now much the same. Thomas released Harley and stepped away—all four men instantly putting their hands in the air—though Eileen hadn't mentioned that as a condition.

Eileen's voice turned icy. "The next person to say a word...or make a wrong move, gets a bullet. It's just as simple as that." The kicker, of course, was no one knew who, exactly, would actually get the bullet. She looked directly at Harley while gesturing with the pistol. "We'll take Charlie's truck," she told the little man. "Go ahead and pull the distributer caps on these others and toss them in the back. Maybe, we can use his radio to keep track of things once we get down below." She inclined her head toward Billy Red Clay's patrol unit. Take those two cans of gas off the back of the cop's truck... I'm thinking they might come in handy."

Harley didn't hesitate; he, too, was sure her near miss was more accident than intent—it was a crap-shoot. Who would catch the next bullet should she pull the trigger again? Eileen had never given him the slightest indication she could shoot. This was just the sort of thing he liked about her; she was a bold and quick thinker.

Harley picked up the folded blanket and basket of food his aunt had left on the tailgate. As he hefted the blanket, he smiled to himself and carried the items to Charlie's truck placing them on the front seat. Going to the other vehicles, he disabled each as instructed. He threw the parts in back with the growing accumulation of other gear—including the supplies Thomas had gathered before leaving home.

Harley did his work methodically, still refusing to consider the consequences of his hastily devised plan.

Eileen had to remind Harley several times they were in a hurry. As he scooped up his friend's handguns, he signaled his agreement and then, smiling apologetically at his friends, he blew the dirt off the pistols and wiped them on his shirt. "I guess you want to take these along don't you, Eileen? And I may as well throw in my shotgun, too. I doubt you want anyone here shooting at us on our way out." Harley seemed almost happy now that he'd set his mind to the thing. He thought if he were going to do this he might as well make a good job of it. After he cuffed Thomas and Charlie Yazzie together through the top bar of Billy Red Clay's brush guard, he used the set of cuffs in Charlie's glove box to fasten Billy alongside them.

Thomas lowered his voice, "Take it easy, Harley. No one wants to get Willie shot," and then whispered, "...and don't throw those keys too far." This, so Harley wouldn't forget and carry them off in his pocket.

Eileen released Harley's Aunt Willie who promised she would not interfere or help the men get loose until after Eileen and Harley were gone. Willie promised she wouldn't, then mouthed a little thanks at her nephew.

Harley reached in his pocket pulling out the handcuff keys and gave them a fling out across the scrub. "You'll probably be able to find those after a bit," he told his aunt. "Maybe the dog can help you. In the meantime you might want to fix these boys a good breakfast so as to take their mind off things." He grinned at his aunt.

Harley then turned to the three men handcuffed to the bumper guard. "I'll drop those truck parts and your guns down the road under the big rock overhang; I wouldn't want you running into Claude Bell with no means of protecting yourselves. When you get loose one of you will have to hike down there and pick the stuff up. By the time you get back Eileen and I should have a pretty good head start."

Willie nodded, gave her nephew a quick hug, and went inside to fix the prisoners something to eat.

Harley and Eileen had barely out of the yard when Grover Etcitty came wandering out of the brush arbor. Pulling up his suspenders, and brushing his hair with his hand, he stopped to look at the men handcuffed to the truck. He was somewhat surprised to see them there. He didn't say anything but stood considering the three for well over a minute then shrugging his shoulders, he went inside for his morning coffee.

18

The Escape

Harley took his time easing around the sandstone slab the police unit had dislodged on its way in that morning. He couldn't imagine how Billy managed to get crosswise of it. Harley suspected more damage was done than just the muffler. That would most likely leave their pursuers only his old pickup for a chase vehicle. Eileen had been smart to choose the Tribal investigator's truck; Charlie was the sort of driver who took good care of a unit. As he reached for the two-way, Harley saw a flicker of mistrust cross Eileen's face. "I thought you wanted to listen to what's going on, Eileen?" Personally, Harley doubted they were close enough to pick up much more than static but felt it wouldn't hurt to have the radio on.

Eileen took her eyes off the horizon to peer across the cab at him, as though seriously considering the question. She looked tired and Harley guessed she'd had no more sleep than him. She turned away finally, closed her eyes, and was silent. He took that to mean she didn't really care, one way or the other, about the two-way radio.

"As soon as we drop off these guns and stuff we'll cut back west again. There are a lot of prospector roads back in this country…uranium and gas mostly. I might be able ta work us out on top—just across from Navajo Mountain. I can't guarantee that…I never heard of anyone trying it…but maybe."

Eileen, now staring straight ahead, remained quiet…wondering where Claude Bell was…if he had been caught…or if he might still be on the loose and just up the road waiting to kill them. *If Harley could keep away from the law why couldn't Claude? He was quite a bit smarter than Harley.*

"Eileen, have you ridden a horse much?"

This brought her to attention. "I'm a town girl, Harley. I've never ridden a horse in my life." She frowned across the cab at him. "Are you thinking that's what it's going to take to make this work?" The thought of making their escape horseback didn't appeal to her in the slightest.

"I'm just thinking, Eileen, that's all. We can't keep this truck of Charlie's very long." He shifted down and canted his head a bit sideways, looking out his side window to scan what little he could see of the sky. "It won't take long this morning 'til they have a plane up here flying this country. This white truck stands out like a sore thumb. Maybe, when we get out from behind this butte, we can pick up some radio reception." He paused a moment to consider what he would do if a plane did appear. "It's not easy to keep from being spotted by an airplane in country like this." Harley then returned to his original thought. "I know an old man, who lives not far from here who runs horses and usually has a few good ones on hand. He owes me a favor from a long time ago." This brought no response, finally prompting Harley to change the subject. "We might yet get some idea what's happening from the two-way." And then almost as an afterthought, "I would kinda' like ta know if they've picked up Claude Bell?"

"You can take care of *him,* can't you, Harley...I mean if we even run into him?" There was a harshness now—an intensity—that made her seem more ominous—dangerous, even. She continued to toy with the pistol making Harley even more anxious. The safety was off. An armed person with no previous shooting experience...and in so obvious a state of agitation...was not to be trifled with in his view. Harley knew, now, Eileen was capable of desperate behavior. Adding a pistol to the mix—and an automatic pistol at that—did not bode well for any sort of negotiation.

Even so, Harley still thought he'd done the right thing back at his Aunt Willie's place, and he intended to help Eileen if he could. This, despite the niggling suspicion there might be some kernel of truth in Billy Red Clay's allegations. There wasn't a whole lot of time left to rethink the thing—not to mention the possibility of making an already sketchy predicament even worse. He knew Thomas and Charlie would come after them with some sort of rescue in mind—at least for him. Billy Red Clay, on the other hand, probably wouldn't hesitate to shoot Eileen should he think the situation warranted it. Harley certainly didn't want to see that happen. He eyed the folded blanket under the food basket and carefully considered his options.

After only a short distance, Harley was able to pick a way down a crooked trail—possibly an abandoned stock drive—into the bottom of a long draw. Heavy brush, tall greasewood, and sage grew along each side of the narrow track, at times crowding right up against the sides of the truck. It was difficult going and he winced as they eased through the dense thicket. Charlie's paint would suffer for this—something the investigator would not likely forget, or forgive, not in any reasonable amount of time.

Without warning, Eileen motioned for him to stop, and with such an urgent look on her face that Harley thought, for a moment, she meant to shoot him right then and there.

"Give me the keys, Harley!" Eileen reached for them as she spoke.

Is this it? Is this the way it will end? Harley's hand inched toward the folded blanket.

"I have to GO, Harley! You know what I mean?" Eileen opened the door and moved into the brush.

Harley watched her disappear into head-high greasewood and reached into the folds of the blanket next to him to remove the hidden 'Long Colt.' After assuring himself the old revolver was, indeed, loaded, he concealed it in the side-pocket of the truck's door, and then clicked on the two-way. After a few seconds of crackling and popping, the radio warmed to a remarkable clarity and Harley heard the strained voice of Billy Red Clay calling for assistance from his damaged patrol unit.

"Roger that, base…we are about…*sizzle, pop, crackle…*"

Apparently, Billy's radio was unable to maintain any sort of contact even with those state agency vehicles manning the checkpoint. Agent Smith, he was sure, didn't know Billy's exact location or how to get there without some additional direction.

Billy tried again and again, but with even less success each time, and soon he was left with nothing more than static to reward his effort. Harley guessed the Navajo policeman was working his two-way radio while Thomas or Charlie hiked to retrieve the distributor parts for the trucks. They were going to be some unhappy boys when they did get on his trail. Harley listened, impressed that Billy's battery had lasted as long as it had. A two-way on transmit sucks up a lot of power and would sap a battery rather quickly from what he'd seen. He, on the other hand, was probably not so far off and he might be able to answer the FBI man himself, but at this point, couldn't think of any reason he should. It was probably best he remain silent—at least until he could get a finer sense of Eileen's thinking. He fiddled with the squelch and wiggled the fine-tuning knob but still could hear nothing beyond static and the whistling moan of atmospheric interference.

Eileen May was nearly back to the vehicle before Harley noticed her coming and quickly hung up the microphone. He left the radio on, but silenced it with the squelch until such time as reception improved. Eileen took a long look around before getting in the truck, reassessing her thinking in regard to their next move. She settled herself in—keeping the automatic handy between her legs—and taking the kinder tact of asking Harley Ponyboy if he wanted to eat a little something before they went on. Not waiting for a reply, she whisked the blanket from under the food basket and tossed it in the back seat. "Let's see what we've got in here?"

Harley eyed the basket and was pleased with his foresight in removing the revolver.

"There's not much in here that I can see, but that's all right I'm sure you'll think of something should we get really hungry."

"I appreciate your confidence on that, Eileen. Thomas brought some canned goods in the toolbox from his house. There's a water jug in the back seat, too, and Charlie always keeps a few emergency supplies back there. I'm sure we'll be fine for a while yet."

Eileen brushed this aside, concentrating instead on unwrapping and passing him one of the peanut butter and jelly sandwiches Willie had packed. She then turned to pull the water jug up front and sat it between them.

Harley glanced across at her. "You might want to put that gun on safety, Eileen. Those automatics are known to go off pretty easy from what I've heard."

Eileen made no move to adjust the gun's safety. "I've been thinking, Harley—what if we just waited them out right here? There's only the top of the truck showing from the air. We could easy break off a little brush to cover that. We'd be pretty much invisible then and we would damn sure be well hidden. I doubt they'll keep those roadblocks up forever. What do you say?"

Harley thought about this new plan and had to admit the idea had merit as long as the food and water held out, and no one stumbled upon them by accident, which he deemed highly unlikely. "I guess it might work, Eileen. The law might eventually figure we made it out another way and head a different direction with the search." Harley didn't really think the FBI would give up quite so easily as that, but who could say? He'd personally seen them do stranger things. In any case he had little in the way of an alternative plan, especially since Eileen had not warmed to the horseback idea. He munched his peanut butter and jelly and sipped from the communal lid of the water jug, all the while throwing Eileen the occasional little smile. This obvious change in her attitude offered hope and he couldn't help having positive thoughts regarding the two of them. Harley, ever the optimist, again found himself on life's brighter path.

19

Armageddon

Charlie Yazzie was not as worried about losing custody of Eileen May as he was about Harley Ponyboy,
and the danger he was exposed to now, having taken
up with the woman. Charlie felt responsible for the
escape; though he couldn't imagine what he might
have done to avoid it. He felt obligated to volunteer
for the not inconsiderable hike to the cache of ignition parts and firearms Harley Ponyboy promised he
would leave behind. Thomas Begay would stay there
to assess which of the remaining vehicles would best
suit their purpose. Thomas was already at it as Charlie started down the road; Billy Red Clay busied
himself trying to get through to the command center
on his radio.

   After giving it a quick once over, Thomas ruled
out the Etcitty's truck, certain the front suspension
had been tweaked to the point of rendering it useless
without major repair. He thought it pretty much the
same story for Billy Red Clay's patrol unit—
probably a waste of time. This left only Harley Ponyboy's old truck: a vehicle he knew to be unreliable at
best. Regardless of which unit was chosen, gas from
the others would have to be siphoned out. This was
not going to be a quick getaway.

Willie's old father, Grover Etcitty, came out of the hogan eating a pudding cup and stood to one side, in quiet contemplation. "You can use my truck." This, with the secret hope of a repair he now suspected might be beyond his ability.

Thomas eyed the old man and shook his head.

Billy Red Clay slammed the door on his tribal unit and said something unintelligible under his breath. "The radio won't get out; I think I might have run the battery down."

Thomas nodded. "Figures," was all he said. "It looks like it's going to be Harley's truck or nothing if we want to get after them in time to do any good. They already have a pretty good jump on us."

Billy sighed and nodded. "How far do you think Charlie had to go to get our stuff?" It had been dark when Billy drove in that morning and he hadn't noticed the rock overhang Harley referred to.

"Not that far, as I recall. Seems to me Harley maybe wanted us to catch up to them. He might have a few doubts about Eileen himself."

Billy gave his uncle a disdainful smile. "Do ya think?"

Thomas Begay only shrugged his shoulders and sniffed. "Harley's pretty far gone on that woman, but he's not an idiot. He might well be coming around."

"I hope so Uncle...but its probable I'll have to arrest him along with her anyway...assuming we catch them." He waved a hand across the canyon. "I know she took him at gunpoint, but to me, he seemed more than willing to go along with her." Billy pondered this further and then went on. "He knows this country better than we do and I suspect he can lose us…should he take a notion. At some point, the FBI are more than likely going to consider him complicit in this thing."

"Harley's a little hardheaded, for sure, but when the chips are down he'll be with us. He was only trying to protect his Aunt Willie." Thomas was not as convinced of this as he sounded, and wished more than ever that Charlie would hurry up with those distributer caps.

Old man Etcitty offered to loan them the battery out of his truck, but neither of the other two responded nor looked his way. Finally, the old man shook his head in disgust and turned back to the hogan. "Willie should have something to eat shortly." He said this more to himself than the other two."

When Willie Etcitty did come to the door and motion them up to the hogan, Thomas was shading his eyes with one hand, watching Charlie Yazzie trudge up the road with a burlap bag in one hand and the two pistols stuck in his belt. Though the morning was still young, and with a decidedly cool breeze from the north, the Legal Services investigator was breathing hard and sweating.

Billy Red Clay moved to his uncle's side and chuckled. "He made pretty good time."

"It wasn't that far…and Charlie does not waste time once he sets his head on a thing."

As Willie passed around a quick breakfast of fried spam on white bread washed down with a large pot of coffee, Thomas Begay got Harley's truck running and Billy filled it with the gas he and Charlie were siphoning from the other trucks.

~~~~~~~

Thomas rubbed his jaw and passed Charlie an old set of binoculars he'd found under the truck seat. To the south, a tangle of canyons and ridges ran to the horizon; it wouldn't take much, he thought, to lose a pickup truck in such country.

Charlie readjusted the focus and blinked a couple of times to clear his vision. "You could hide a herd of elephants down there," he said, as he scanned a small segment just to the east of the greater basin, then zeroed in on something moving along the edge of an arroyo. He watched as a coyote lifted his nose and tested the breeze.

"See something?" Thomas followed the direction Charlie was looking. "I don't see anything."

Billy Red Clay, too, was watching, and even from this distance, his younger eyes told him it was Old Man Coyote attracting the investigator's interest.

Charlie leaned forward, as though a few inches might make a difference, finally deciding Coyote was only conducting business as usual and showed no particular sense of anxiety. That was good enough for him and he moved his search area farther toward the horizon. It was impossible to discern much, in the way of details, at that distance but he immediately picked up a trail of dust against the clear blue of the morning sky. He was unable to make much of it, but from experience, figured it for a fast moving vehicle, meaning it was likely on a service road possibly one pushed back in to a distant well-head. He passed the glasses to Billy Red Clay.

"See if you can figure out what's making that dust... the other side of the basin...just there, on the horizon." Charlie pointed toward the smudge as best he could, but without the glasses, quickly lost track.

Billy, readjusting the focus, shook his head, unable to identify the source of the wavering plume of dust.

Thomas Begay strained his eyes in that direction as well, but was unable to see anything of the sort.

When Billy did finally locate the telltale dust, he murmured, "Someone seems to be in a pretty big hurry to get somewhere...or maybe just anywhere." He said this last with a glance at his uncle, but implying nothing beyond the stated fact.

Thomas cleared his throat, "Well, it's a long way off and would take a while for us to get over there—if it's even possible to get over there from here." He snorted. "You'd a thought one of us would have remembered to bring a topo map of this country."

Charlie rubbed his eyes where the binoculars had left dark circles from the black rubber eyecups. "I did bring a topo map—it's in my truck—Harley has it now."

"That's just great; the one man who doesn't need a topo out here is the only man that has one." This made Thomas smile in spite of himself. The other two looked at one another for a moment and then all three were smiling. The *Dinés'* keen sense of self-deprecating humor kicked in. Their people had always taken a certain pleasure in jokes...even if they *were* on themselves.

"One thing's for certain, sooner or later, Harley and the woman have to show up. The FBI casts a big net when they get serious…and I think they are serious now." Charlie was fairly certain of this. He was already thinking there was air surveillance on the way.

"Well, you'd guess so wouldn't you?" Thomas wasn't so certain as his friend.

Billy Red Clay, who was still looking through the glasses, suddenly said, "Uh oh."

Thomas came to attention and looked in the same direction. "What?" he leaned forward, almost touching the windshield.

Billy didn't say anything for a moment but when Charlie nudged him he turned and said, "I think maybe that vehicle is slowing down." The policeman grew even more intent. "He's pulled into a clump of cedars." Billy was excited now. "I wouldn't have seen him at all if the light hadn't been just right."

Thomas narrowed an eye in that direction. "There *are* people living out here you know, not many, but a few. It could be a woodcutter or…who the hell knows who it could be." Thomas held out his hand for his nephew to pass the binoculars. Readjusting the focus he nodded slowly as he picked up the vehicle. "It's not Charlie's Chevy, that's for sure. It's a dark color… dark gray, maybe. Too far to see if anyone's around…I don't see anything moving now." He fiddled with the focus, "I could be wrong, but it looks to me like it could be the truck that was following us last night."

Nothing they saw could be considered out of the ordinary yet the men were immediately on their mettle. No one said anything for several minutes as each privately considered what options were left.

Thomas trained the binoculars slightly more to the east and played them over the lower, more gentle terrain in the direction of the highway. "You know...there seems to be some kind of stock drive or the like...and not too far from here. Looks like it might eventually take a person over into the basin." He paused and studied the area more closely before putting the binoculars down. "You never know though...it wouldn't take much to get rimmed up in this country." He then, as best he could, committed the location of the now abandoned gray pickup to memory.

Charlie Yazzie started the truck and pointed it east, thinking, *The only chance of finding Harley Ponyboy out here...is if he wants to be found.*

~~~~~~~~~

Harley Ponyboy woke with a start, snorted and sniffed; the breeze through the window was starting to cool and the cab of the truck, now covered in brush, had fallen under the lazy aura of late afternoon. Eileen, when he looked over, also appeared to be asleep but with the slitted eyes of someone only dozing, still aware, on some level, of her surroundings. The fingers of one hand lie across the automatic pistol at her side—the side opposite Harley—and he cringed to see the weapon perched so precariously at the edge of the seat. He stared at the red dot below the slide, indicating it was ready to fire. It might take only the twitch of a finger or the slight jolt of a fall to bring it to life.

Eileen May opened one eye a little wider, slowly turned to look at him, and stretched one shoulder, then the other, before taking a firmer grip on the pistol. "I could use a little drink of whiskey."

Harley sighed, and then nodded, finally. "Me too." He rubbed his jaw. "It's probably a good thing we don't have one." When he heard no confirmation, he looked directly at her. "Are you sure you want to ride this thing out right here?"

Eileen looked out the window and didn't say anything. *There is nothing to see...and nothing to say.*

At his open window, Harley, listened to a dozen little sounds; some of which his mind automatically recognized and dismissed...but not all. Twice now he thought he'd heard a truck far in the distance. *Sound in this country tends to travels a long way under the right conditions,* he thought. But even if this *was* what he heard, it was not close enough to be considered a problem—too far off and in the wrong direction to concern them for now. The other sound, and this *did* bother him, was the muffled roll of distant thunder—very far away—and probably too much to the north, he thought, to pose any great threat to their little hideout. Thunder can be deceiving, especially in canyon country, where it should never be ignored. A typical summer downpour anywhere in the vast drainage above them, might send a wall of water crashing their way in less time than can be imagined. Flash floods are a danger to be guarded against in that, sometimes chancy and always unpredictable, land.

Eileen, too, sat still, listening, hearing nothing she recognized as threatening. Turning to him, she asked. "Are you hungry, again? This might be a good time to have a little more to eat." She said this while eyeing Willie Etcitty's food basket for the second time since they'd left camp.

"Eileen, did you have anything to do with killing that old man?" Harley could not bear the burden of it any longer and did not know how else to say it.

She pursed her lips and looked long and hard at the little man: then waving a hand in dismissal she asked. "What do you think, Harley…do you think I killed him?" She smiled, a winsome little smile that gave little hint of an answer.

"Why did you decide to make a run for it…if you didn't have a hand in it?"

"That Tribal cop, Billy Red Clay, was convinced I was part of it. I could hear it in his voice. He would have arrested me in a heartbeat. Once they had me, they would never let me off. They would pin it on me no matter what. I couldn't take that chance. If they were unable to catch Claude, they would set me up for it, that's a given…and even if they do catch him, he would be first to throw me under the bus. I do know that about him." She shook her head. "No…I'll take my chances out here; you'll come up with something."

"So, what did happen?" Harley wasn't sure he wanted to know, but the uncertainty was killing him.

Eileen turned away and stared out through the brush piled on the hood. A small bird came to light on a twig above them and looked in, directly at her, one bright little eye cocked, as though he, too, was waiting to hear. In an instant, he was gone. Free, she thought…as only a little bird can be.

"I was ahead of Claude that night, but not by much, and when my last ride let me off...somewhere across the New Mexico state line...I was left with my thumb out again.

What with the rain and all, I couldn't see who was driving the old truck when it stopped. I was nearly halfway in before he turned and I saw it was Claude. He grabbed my arm and I fought him, but he held tight till he thought we were moving too fast for me to jump out. I knew, then, I couldn't get away without being killed. Either way, I was going to be dead. Oh, I knew he intended killing me all right. I had almost decided I would rather jump when he ordered me to look in the glove box and see if there was a road map or something to tell us where we were and how far to the next town."

Eileen took a deep breath, holding it an interminable minute, before finally exhaling. "I guess the mind welcomes any sort of distraction when hope is gone. There wasn't any map...only a paper bag, and behind that this pistol." She caressed the little automatic as she said this, and lifted it to the light to better admire her salvation. "I pulled it out and stuck it in his face; it almost caused a wreck he was so surprised. I didn't know if it was loaded or not, but saw pretty quick that *he* thought it was, and that's when I knew I had him. We were coming up on a wide spot and I told him to pull over. Then I said, 'Get out of the truck or die where you set!' He knew I meant it, too, and obviously preferred getting out. The last I saw of him, he was standing in the rain with a weird little smile on his face. He shook his finger at me a time or two and I knew then, he would come after me.

213

I should have shot him when I had the chance…and would have…if I had been certain the gun would fire."

When she stopped to catch her breath, Harley reached over and patted her shoulder. "That must have been terrible. Eileen. I cannot imagine how you got through it." He meant it, too, and was left even more in awe of the woman.

"Well, anyway, I blew straight through Shiprock, and when I got to Farmington, I took to the side streets to find a place to leave the truck." She shuddered. "I didn't know at the time that Claude had killed the old man, but I had a pretty good idea he hadn't come by that truck in any good way. I just knew I didn't want to be caught with it…and I damn sure didn't want to stick around Farmington where he could find me." Eileen nervously licked her lips, and not thinking, laid the gun down between them; so intent was she on how Harley was taking her story.

"I found a vacant lot and parked the truck, cleaning off my prints as best I could. I knew better than leave anything that could tie me to a stolen vehicle. It was then I remembered the paper bag I'd seen in the glove-box; something told me I should have a look. When I pulled it out it didn't take long to see it was money. I still have almost all of it…several thousand dollars, I guess." Here she stopped to see if Harley had anything to say about the money.

He didn't. In fact, it hardly registered at all; his mind was racing far ahead of her story.

Eileen, encouraged by his silence, went on. "I assumed, later, when we heard about the killing on the radio, that Claude had only taken what the old man had in his pocket. He was probably so fixed on getting away he hadn't taken time to search the truck. I'd only walked a few blocks down the street when I saw a man getting out of his pickup to stretch, and then take a drink from a bottle. I could see he had spent the night in the truck. As I passed him, I stopped to ask if he was headed out of town. He said, yes. He had been drinking most of the night and was heading home. That man was Alfred Nakii; he had a gentle voice...it was his bad luck to offer me a ride." Eileen's voice trailed off...she looked at Harley Ponyboy in such a way he could almost hear her say... *"You know the rest."*

The two, eyes locked, and intent only on what the other might be thinking, were still immersed in the story, and didn't notice the figure at the window. Harley saw Eileen's eyes widen just as he felt a firm grip on his shoulder. He instinctively grabbed the gun from the seat and was bringing it to bear on the intruder when he heard Thomas's voice—calm and low.

"Just be glad it's me and not Claude Bell."

When he realized who it was, Harley was indeed glad, but couldn't help saying, "...and you better be glad I didn't shoot you!" He turned to look at his friend and then glanced in the side mirror to see Billy Red Clay, with his gun drawn and leveled, and Charlie Yazzie, standing askance, staring at the damage to the paint on his truck. Charlie's .38 hung loose at his side, and it occurred to Harley he might yet have a shot or two flung at him. Harley reached for Eileen, taking her wrist to prevent any instinctive move toward making a run for it and possibly catching a bullet in the process. Officer Red Clay was not of a nature to set aside protocol. It was...who he was.

~~~~~~~

Harley faced his captors and was adamant he didn't want *his* truck left behind.

"Someone might steal it," the little man cautioned, looking suspiciously in every direction.

Thomas laughed and shook his head. "Harley...in the first place...no one else would want it. And in the second place: the two most likely to steal it are already under arrest."

Harley wasn't amused and glared back, asking, "How did you find us out here anyway?" He made certain to say this loudly enough for Eileen to hear.

Thomas first looked incredulous, but quick to catch on, whispered back, "I think you know how we found you, Harley. Once you turned off on that stock driveway you weren't hard to follow. Those big tires of Charlie's leave tracks that are pretty easy to spot." Both men glanced sideways at the woman, satisfied Eileen couldn't hear them. "I knew you were laying a trail, Harley."

On the way back out to the highway, and what Billy Red Clay was now calling Checkpoint Charlie, the fugitives went back over the story Eileen had so recently related to Harley. Both lawmen were taking mental notes with a view to their later written reports.

The Tribal policeman sat in back with Eileen and Harley sat up front with the Legal Services investigator. Billy hadn't cuffed either of them, but only with the understanding, he would before they reached search headquarters; it would be expected, he said.

On their way in, Charlie, spent a good deal of time on the radio letting Fred Smith of the FBI know they were on their way in with prisoners, and giving the agent a preliminary report on the morning's activities. He made sure Tribal Policeman Billy Red Clay received credit for the arrests. Billy, of course, protested, but Charlie thought it only right the young officer be redeemed after letting Harley and Eileen get away in the first place—at least, that's how Captain Beyale would see it. Charlie didn't want Billy left holding the bag.

FBI Agent Fred Smith was first to meet them. Fred accepted the prisoners in handcuffs as was proper and, overall, was happy enough with how things turned out. His superiors, he thought, would be pleased as well. It had been a very full day for the newly appointed federal agent and he was generous with his praise of everyone who'd had a hand in the outcome—Charlie Yazzie included.

The FBI man tried to sound matter-of-fact as he waved an arm toward the tented command post, surprising everyone by saying, "We have Claude Bell. He only made it about eight or nine miles west of here. He was already in the backcountry before we even set up our roadblock. We had, of course, taken that possibility into consideration and still doubted he could work his way back past us...and he didn't." Here the FBI man couldn't help smiling. "His truck apparently ran out of gas leaving him afoot in a very rough area. A fly-over by federal wildlife officers spotted the truck and reported a man fitting Bell's description running from the abandoned vehicle."

The FBI man paused a moment and looked around the group.

"Fortunately, one of our search volunteers, a Navajo park ranger from up at Monument Valley happened to be closest and heard the report. When he tracked him down, he said Bell had fallen off a ledge and was pretty beat up, disoriented, dehydrated, and nearly unconscious." The FBI man grimaced. "The ranger figured he better get him back here for medical attention without waiting for an emergency crew to try and find their way back in there.

Our EMT said the man was in a very bad way and appeared to be unconscious. He's working on him in the tent right now."

Harley looked over at Eileen and saw her slump, lowering her head as though she might be sick. He moved to support her, and Charlie went to fetch a cup of water from the little table under the tent fly. As he was filling the paper cup a man with a stethoscope over his shoulder came out and looked around for Agent Smith.

"Have you seen the guy in charge?" He asked.

Charlie paused and took the cup from the spigot. "I believe he's over there," he said, pointing Smith out. "How's the patient, Doc?"

"That's what I need to see him about. I'm afraid he got to us too late. The man's dead. He was nearly so when they brought him in. I didn't think he would make it even then." The medical technician murmured almost to himself, "He looked more like he'd taken a beating instead of just a fall."

Charlie, already turned to go, canted his head at this and turned again to face the technician, "Where is the ranger who brought him in?"

"That, I don't know. He helped us take the stretcher into the tent and then said he had to get back up to Monument Valley."

Charlie walked over and peeked inside the tent. "Has anyone identified your guy in here yet?"

"No. The FBI agent looked in on him when he was first brought in; that was just before you people arrived. He had a rough fax picture with him but you couldn't tell much from it. This guy's face is so beat up I doubt his own mother would recognize him."

"I'll tell the agent in charge," Charlie said over his shoulder as he strode off with the cup of water.

Fred Smith, still filling out arrest forms for Harley and Eileen, trying to hold the papers down on his car's fender; a breeze had come up making it hard to keep anything in place.

Charlie walked over and handed Eileen the water, then motioned for Harley to help her with it before moving over next to Fred and waiting for him to look up.

"What?" Fred asked.

"Your suspect is dead," Charlie said. "The EMT just told me."

Fred, put the back of his hand to his forehead, rubbing one side then the other, reflecting on the implications of this; certainly, it would make things easier as far as presenting trial evidence...and it would save the taxpayers money, too. Fred had little compassion for men like Claude Bell.

Charlie hesitated before going on—not sure how the agent might take his next question. "The EMT...he said the suspect hadn't really been identified as yet?"

"My God, Charlie, they just brought him in a few minutes before you pulled up. The State Patrol is already standing down and lifting the road blocks—what are you saying?"

"I understand all that, Fred, it's just... Do we even know who we have in there... I mean for sure?"

Charlie had the agent's full attention now and he watched as a look of disbelief flickered across the man's face.

Fred pulled a folded fax paper from his pocket and passed it to the Tribal investigator. "No one up here has ever seen this guy; this fax picture isn't much help, as you can see."

Charlie studied the picture and had to admit the quality of the fax made it nearly impossible to identify anyone by it.

"Well, we have someone here, now, who does know him." Both men turned to look at Eileen who was sipping water and talking quietly to Harley Ponyboy. Harley hovered over her, patting her shoulder occasionally despite the handcuffs. He seemed to be assuring her everything would be all right—something he had no way of knowing and that was reflected in Eileen's face. She looked up as the two lawmen approached and even Billy Red Clay, who was keeping a close eye on the pair, knew something was up.

Fred Smith didn't quite know how to begin, but as was his wont, approached it straight on. "Eileen, we have been informed the person we think is Claude Bell, didn't make it. I'm afraid we are going to need your help…much as I hate to ask at a time like this. We would appreciate it if you could take a look at the body inside and see if you can make a positive identification. It's just a formality, but we'd like to go ahead and do it now. It will save you the trouble of having to face it later. I know it's a lot to ask but I will be sure to note your cooperation in your file. That could be very helpful for you, Eileen."

Eileen had partially regained her composure but now had to take a breath or two to keep from losing it again. She nodded and with Harley supporting her on one side, and Charlie on the other, they made their way to the tent. Agent Smith led the way and Thomas Begay brought up the rear along with his nephew, Billy Red Clay, neither of whom had any desire to see a dead person.

When they entered the tent, all but Thomas and Billy, the EMT was just finishing up his work; he'd removed the IV and placed a sheet over the remains. Seeing what the little group was about, he waited until they were gathered around and then pulled back the top half of the sheet. Eileen paled but remained strangely quiet as she stared at the person on the gurney. In death, the swelling had gone down somewhat and she studied the face carefully before looking directly at Fred Smith.

"This is not Claude Bell," she said before anyone else could speak. "I'm certain of it. It's not him." She turned away and looked up to the canvas ceiling for a moment, tears forming at the corners of her eyes.

R. Allen Chappell

Harley Ponyboy, still staring at the corpse, made a little sound in his throat. "I know who it is...and it's not Claude Bell."

Charlie gave his friend an odd look. "Harley you've never seen Claude Bell; how could you know it's not him?"

Harley's face fell apart. "Cause it's my cousin, Jimmy Tall Horse. He's a park ranger over in Tsé Bii' Ndzisgaii...we were good friends when we were kids. I haven't seen him in a few years...but... it's him all right."

"Sonofabitch!" No one there had ever heard Fred Smith curse, but under the circumstances, they were not surprised when he did. The lawman appeared stunned and shook his head in disbelief.

Billy Red Clay shook his head as well. "We better get on the horn and see if we can catch those state patrolmen." He cleared his throat. "Anyone know which direction the bastard went when he pulled out?"

The EMT, replacing the sheet, thought for a moment and said, "North toward Blanding." He lived in Monticello, himself, and remembered wishing he could be heading that direction too.

Fred Smith pulled himself together in a matter of seconds, and was once again the ever capable FBI agent everyone expected him to be. "Billy, radio Tribal and let them know the suspect is still at large. I'll have the state patrol inform their people to be on the alert." Fred was back up to speed, and once again, determined to apprehend Claude Bell at any cost—knowing full well now his career might depend on it. "Billy, you are going to have to transport these two prisoners back to Farmington. We can't have them standing around out here…and we can't just pack them around with us either."

Billy was about to protest the assignment when he saw the look on the agent's face, and knew it was useless. The FBI was in charge of this investigation and he was at their mercy.

Charlie could see Agent Smith was about to give chase and approached him from a different angle. "Fred, Bell has the ranger's truck, and if he decides to go off-road again, you won't be able to follow in your car…not for very far anyway."

Fred immediately saw the wisdom in this and didn't hesitate when he said. "I'll borrow *your* truck then. He can't be far; it's only been fifteen or twenty minutes. I still have a shot at catching up."

"No. Thomas and I are taking my truck but you can come along if you like." Charlie's tone left no room for argument.

This confounded the FBI man but he could see Charlie, too, was determined, and while he had the authority to commandeer the truck, he didn't have time for the hassle. A confrontation now might have later ramifications.

"Let's go," he sighed, finally, then turned to the government car where he opened the trunk. He selected an assault rifle and a short-barreled shotgun— and ammunition belts to go with them.

Charlie and Thomas stood watching as the agent loaded everything in the truck and beckoned them over. "I see you have extra gas cans in back," the agent smiled at this. "I doubt Bell has any extra. In fact, that ranger's truck should be a little low on fuel by now." The agent stopped and stared at the two for a moment as though judging just how far to go. "I mean to bring this man in one way or the other. If we're going, let's be gone."

Thomas smiled at this; it was his kind of talk and coming from a lawman, he found it refreshing, to say the least.

Charlie was thinking...*We don't know if Bell is armed. I didn't see a gun belt on that park ranger, and I'm pretty sure they carry.*

20

The Fatalist

Claude Bell had long been of the opinion he was a good bit smarter than the average lawman, and occasionally, even thought he might have made a good officer himself...should things have been different. He'd been raised on a reservation: Oklahoma and the Choctaw Nation. But that was a different sort of life from that led by these Indians out here. The Navajo people were a breed apart from those farther to the east...or maybe it was his white blood that made it seem so.

Eileen understood him, at least she appeared to, at first. He figured, both of them being half-breeds, gave them something in common. That hadn't gone anywhere. Still, he had to admit he'd been lucky, luckier than he had any right to be, in fact. That park ranger had come within a whit of catching him out. He'd heard him coming just in time to step behind an outcrop of rock and wait. When he smashed him in the face with a jagged piece of rock he felt the man's septum give way and knew, then, he had little to worry about from that quarter. It was while he was relieving the ranger of his gun belt, the idea struck him. The man was about his size and weight. They didn't look anything alike in the face, but that could be remedied. It would be dangerous, to be sure, but everything he did, of late, was more or less dangerous.

A man surviving on the outskirts of society had to be bold, and of an adventurous nature if he were to make a go of such a life. There was nothing else for it.

When Claude arrived at the check station in the ranger's uniform—the Navajo park ranger—bloody and unconscious—was dressed in Claude's clothes. The EMT met them at the vehicle and the two of them put the injured man on the gurney and got him inside. Claude was sure his victim couldn't speak and doubted he would last long enough to be a problem.

Fred Smith was on the radio at the time and when he was finally able to head that way, the park ranger's four-wheel-drive was already pulling out on the highway. The driver didn't look back and the federal agent, being more interested in the fugitive, went directly to the tent and the injured prisoner.

Yes...it had all gone rather well, in Claude's opinion. There had been plenty of time since his report of the apprehension that the roadblocks should already be down, and in this, he was proven correct. The gas gauge showed little fuel remaining, that was true, but he figured he still could make it to Monticello and fill up there. He was making good time when he felt the thump of a tire going flat. But still, he was not worried; it would take only a few minutes to change the tire and he would be on his way. *Nothing was ever easy.*

Putting on the spare took a little longer than Claude anticipated, but not so long as to worry him much. He felt he had a pretty good cushion, time wise, and the last thing he wanted to do was get in a hurry—that would only make for more problems. He crossed the Utah State Line and drove through the small town of Bluff, but the one service station there was closed. Glancing at the park ranger's map he saw Blanding ahead with renewed hope for fuel. But, as he slowed at the Quick Stop there, he noticed another park ranger's truck fueling. This section of Utah was host to a number of state and national parks and he suspected many of the ranger's knew one another. He didn't want to risk being discovered when he was doing so well. He waved at the ranger in passing. It would be Monticello for fuel.

As the truck climbed out on top of the next mesa, Claude found a greener, more hospitable, landscape. He relaxed, a little, and even enjoyed the scenery and cooler air of the higher elevation. The two-way radio was on and he adjusted the squelch, as he had several times already, but there was nothing more than a light atmospheric static to reward his efforts. If his luck held, he would be in Colorado by morning, and eventually Denver, where he would have some people-cover and not feel so exposed. The map noted a turn off at LaSalle junction with Highway 46 heading east and into Colorado the back way. It was a very isolated part of the country and looked much the better prospect when compared to I-70, which, he guessed, would be well patrolled.

Monticello was a welcome surprise when it came in view. For the last ten miles he felt he was running on fumes and that was making him anxious. He fueled without incident and was happy he had waited.

He'd have enough now to make it straight through Gateway to Grand Junction.

It was falling dark, and Claude was almost to his turnoff when he noticed the glow of headlights in his rearview mirror. There had been very little traffic the last fifty miles or so. He slowed, slightly, making sure he was just below the speed limit—too slow, he knew, would attract nearly as much attention as going too fast: not a good thing at this stage of the game. As the headlights grew slightly brighter, he realized the other vehicle was gaining fast and would soon overtake him. For no reason at all, a chill fell across him. Intuition perhaps—it almost never failed him—and this time was strong enough to send an icy finger down his back. He kicked his speed up a notch and still the other vehicle stayed with him. Now, when he slowed, the other vehicle slowed as well. His turnoff was only a mile or so farther and that would tell the tale. Yes…it could be a local who lived at LaSalle but it was unlikely, he thought. He slowed for the turn and the other followed suit. A cool breeze filled the cab as he rolled the window down and watched in his side mirror hoping the other vehicle would turn into the scatter of houses just off the highway. Claude floored the truck and headed for the winding road down the imposing cliffs to the isolated and lonely Paradox Valley.

The road hadn't looked that bad on the map and Claude Bell hadn't a clue as to how dangerous its twisty turns and sudden drop-offs could be.

~~~~~~

Thomas Begay shouted. "That's him up ahead! I know it is!" Charlie Yazzie and FBI Agent Smith were taken aback at the outburst; every car they came up on was suspect, of course, but they could see no indication this particular vehicle in front of them was their man, not at this distance. Both looked at Thomas. Charlie shook his head, peered into the night, and was dubious. "There's no way to tell that from here."

"Yes, there is. When that park truck pulled out of the checkpoint, I noticed its exhaust was smoking... white like that truck up ahead; there's still a haze laying on the road." Thomas was convinced and Charlie knew he was the sort who would notice such a thing.

"See those taillights? Late model Dodge pickup taillights—that park truck was a Dodge. This is it, I tell you." Thomas was clearly excited now and it was infectious.

Charlie tromped the accelerator, and as they pulled closer, could more clearly see the smoke. Charlie backed off and the Dodge slowed slightly as well. He looked over at the FBI man.

"What do you think, Fred?"

"Let's ease back a bit and follow him for a few minutes." The FBI man was well schooled in the artifices of pursuit.

Thomas was having a hard time containing himself, gripping the dash with both hands, and again shouted, "Stay with him, Charlie! We've got him now."

Fred Smith leaned forward as well. "Hit your lights and siren, Charlie. Let's see if he'll pull over."

When the lights and siren came on, the Dodge only increased its speed, though they were already hitting eighty after the long downhill straightaway. Less than a mile farther on the truck, without using it's turn signals, suddenly dived to the right and skidded the rear end sideways as it made the turn onto 46, slowing very little for the first of the gentle curves. Charlie began to lose ground. Fred, who was a standout of the FBI's driving school at Quantico, could see what was happening and gently began to coach him. "Brake hard before the curves, Charlie, then accelerate into them."

Thomas had been on this road several times when he worked in the oilfield and was nearly breathless when he said, "He's going way too fast. There's some bad curves at the top of the bluff. Ease off, Charlie. I don't think he's going to make it."

The words hardly left Thomas's mouth when the switchbacks began to tighten, and they could see, by the taillights, the truck was fishtailing, trying to hold traction in the turns. About that time, the highway straightened slightly and they could see the lights pull away—and then disappear.

"Don't worry, Charlie! There's a twenty-mile stretch of straight road at the bottom. We'll catch him there. He can't outrun this Chevy down on the flats."

At the edge of the bluff, Charlie slowed considerably, and as they started down Thomas held up a hand.

"Stop!' There was a light haze of dust in the air and skid marks across the gravel to the edge. Thomas nodded. "I didn't think he would make it."

The three of them got down from the truck and walked through the dust to the edge. Fred Smith stood at the brink of the nothingness, and in his matter of fact way, said, "We got him all right."

Far below, possibly more than a thousand feet by the time the truck tumbled over and over across the broken sandstone at the bottom, there was only the glow from one headlight to mark the truck's final resting place…and that, too, soon disappeared.

Charlie's heart was pounding so hard he thought, *surely the others can hear it*. He searched the darkness about them. "You don't think he could have jumped out, do you?" He couldn't imagine it, but had to at least explore the possibility.

Thomas stepped even closer to the edge, and peered out into the night and the twinkling lights of the tiny settlement of Paradox. He spit into the void. "He didn't jump out. He didn't have time to *even think* about jumping out."

Fred Smith nodded agreement. "We better call into Moab for a recovery team. This is going to take awhile."

~~~~~~~

It was nearly daylight when Charlie Yazzie drove up the road to his house. Already, the guinea hens were coming down from the neighbor's trees, marshaling their forces into tight little bands of marauders, eager to begin another day's adventure. Guineas live a precarious life and like to get the most from what time they have.

R. Allen Chappell

The light had been left on in the living room and Charlie knew Sue was probably already up and in the kitchen.

She was at the door before he could turn off the truck. Smiling, she asked, "Shall we run to greet the sun this morning?"

Charlie gave a tired smile in return. "I'll be lucky if I can make it into the house this morning."

Sue laughed and said, "I knew you were on the way. Lucy Tallwoman called to say you dropped Thomas off at their place and were headed home. It sounded like you two had quite a night?"

"Is the coffee on?" Charlie put his arm around his wife and they were soon at the table with steaming cups before them.

Sue gave him a minute to settle himself and fix his coffee. After a few sips, her husband seemed inclined to talk and she pulled her chair closer.

It took Charlie nearly an hour to fill her in on the night's happenings. Sue didn't interrupt, and at the end, was left wide-eyed and filled with questions. "Where are Harley and that woman, Eileen, now?"

"They are both in holding, waiting to see what charges, if any, might be filed by the federal prosecutor. After I have breakfast, and get cleaned up, I'll meet with Fred Smith and we'll see what's to be done." He paused. "If Claude Bell had lived, it would be a totally different story. Eileen would be in custody as a material witness, taken to Phoenix, and held at the discretion of the prosecutor down there. As it is, Fred and I believe she'll more than likely be arraigned here on the reservation and go before a Tribal judge on reduced charges. Her mother's a Navajo and that means she's a Navajo. Unless Willie Etcitty and her father decide to press charges for stealing their pickup…which is not likely."

"What about Harley?"

"Harley had no knowledge of any criminal activity on Eileen's part…so no harboring of a fugitive. Fred and Billy Red Clay agree he was coerced, and forced against his will to go with her on her escape. Billy argued for a kidnapping charge at first but his Uncle Thomas talked him out of that saying it would serve no purpose at this point. Harley wouldn't have gone along with it anyway. He said he enjoyed the whole thing and would testify on her behalf should it come to that. We'll get it all sorted out this morning. There'll be official depositions taken by the Bureau in regard to the murder down in Arizona, but with Claude Bell out of the picture, she shouldn't have to appear in person down there. Fred thinks it should, pretty much, be case closed for the Phoenix Bureau. And, in the end, it should be pretty much the same for the Benny Klee case here on the reservation.

"What about her and Harley? Are they involved…uh, a couple now… or what?"

"Now, *that*, we don't know…and I'm not sure they know either. Harley would be up for it…I'm guessing here…but Eileen is a hard one to figure. We'll just have to wait and see, I suppose. She is on the Navajo Tribal Rolls and eligible to receive help or assistance here on the reservation, but we'll just have to see how that plays out. I think it might be good for Harley if she stayed on…but it's anyone's guess if that will happen."

"And what about Thomas's father? Do they know yet if Bell had anything to do with his death?" Sue had been thinking about Thomas and his relationship with his father, and was hopeful their friend might find some sort of closure in all that had happened.

"Fred isn't sure if we'll ever know if Bell was involved in Gilbert's death. Something might have come out if the case had gone to trial, but probably not now." Charlie wagged his head. "Thomas, of course, is convinced Bell had something to do with it. But proving it in a court of law would be another matter." Charlie slurped the rest of his coffee, kissed his wife on the forehead and headed to the shower, leaving Sue to ponder and fill in the gaps for herself.

~~~~~~

It was Harley Ponyboy himself who took Eileen May to the bus station in Farmington. He'd offered to drive her all the way to Utah and the little town outside Salt Lake where her aunt lived. She declined, saying it was better they not do that. "It would just make it that much harder," she said.

Harley nodded. "Maybe in the fall...Eileen, after you are settled in...maybe then, I could come for a visit?"

"Maybe so, Harley. It's not that far. I'll be in touch...who knows..."

When the bus pulled up in a cloud of diesel fumes, Eileen picked up her shoulder bag and took out a Bible. "I want you to have this, Harley...you know...just in case you ever have need of one."

They both smiled as Harley took the Bible and nodded thoughtfully. "What if *you* need it, Eileen? I'll always have it should you want it back"

She smiled, "We'll see Harley...we'll see." She leaned over, gave him a kiss on the cheek, and turned to hand the driver her ticket.

On the bus, Eileen took a window seat and rummaged around in her bag for her transfer from Salt Lake to Seattle, Washington. *It should be some cooler up there this time of year,* she thought, as she turned to the window where Harley Ponyboy stood waving goodbye. She smiled and waved back. *Poor Harley—he doesn't know how lucky he is.*

She fluffed up the tiny white pillow on the headrest thinking a short nap would be good. She hadn't been able to sleep lately; she couldn't get old Benny Klee, lying there dead in the mud, out of her mind.

R. Allen Chappell

ABOUT THE AUTHOR

R. Allen Chappell's work has appeared in magazines, literary and poetry publications, and been featured on public radio and television. He is the author of seven novels and a collection of short stories, Fat of the Land. All of his work is now available in seven different countries. He grew up in New Mexico, spent a good portion of his life at the edge of the great reservation, and still lives not so far from there.

For the curious, the author's random thoughts on each book are listed below in the order of their release:

Navajo Autumn

It was not my original intent to write a series but this first book was so well received, and with so many readers asking for another, I finally decided to write a sequel—after that there was no turning back. I'm sure I made every mistake a writer can possibly make in a first novel, but I had the advantage of a dedicated little group of detractors, quick to point out its many deficiencies...and I thank them. Without their help, that first book would doubtless have languished, eventually sinking into the morass and there would be no series. The book has, over the years, been through many editions and updates. I know, now, how to make this an even better book and someday I might. But for now, I will leave it as it is. No book is perfect, and this one keeps me centered.

Boy Made of Dawn

A sequel I very much enjoyed writing and one that drew many new fans to the series. So many, in fact, I quit my day job to pursue writing these stories full-time—not a course I would ordinarily recommend to an author new to the process. In this instance, however, it proved to be the right move. As I learn, I endeavor to make each new book a little better...and to keep their prices low enough that people like me can afford to read them.

Ancient Blood

The third book in the series and the initial flight into the realm of Southwestern archaeology. This book introduced Harley Ponyboy: a character who quickly carved out a major niche for himself in all the stories that followed. Harley remains the favorite of reservation readers to this day. Also debuting in this novel was Professor George Armstrong Custer, noted archaeologist and Charlie Yazzie's old professor at UNM. He, too, has a pivotal role in some of the later books.

Mojado

This book was a departure for the series in cover art, subject matter, and its move to thriller status on Amazon.com. A story built around a local tale heard in Mexico many years ago. In the first three months following release, this book sold more copies, and faster, than any of the previous books. It's still a personal favorite of mine.

Magpie Speaks

A mystery/thriller that goes back to the beginning and exposes the past of several major characters some of which play pivotal roles in later books in the series. This book has become another favorite of Navajo friends who follow these stories.

Wolves of Winter

As our readership attained a solid position in the gen-re, I decided to tell the story I had, for many years, envisioned. I am pleased with its success on several levels, and in very different genres. I hope one day to revisit this story in one form or another.

The Bible Seller

Another cultural departure, in which Harley Ponyboy, once again, wrests away the starring role. A story of attraction and deceit told against a backdrop of wanton murder and reservation intrigue. It promises to be yet another Canyon-lands favorite.

From the Author

Readers may be pleased to know they can preview various audio book selections for the Navajo Nation Series on our book pages, also in public libraries, on Audible, and in many retail outlets. Kaipo Schwab, an accomplished actor and storyteller, narrates the audio books. I am pleased Kaipo felt these books worthy of his considerable talent.

There are more books in the planning stage and one already in progress. Happily, our reader base increases daily and all indicators remain positive for the series to continue with stories of our favorite denizens of the Navajo Nation. I hope you enjoy these adventures as much as I enjoy bringing them to you. We remain available to answer questions, and welcome your comments at: rachappell@yahoo.com

The author and his wife call Western Colorado home. From here in the High Desert, he continues to pursue a lifelong interest in the prehistory of the Four Corners region and its people.

If you've enjoyed this book, please consider going to our book page to leave a short review. It takes only a minute and would be most appreciated.

R. Allen Chappell

Glossary

1. *Adáánii* — undesirable, alcoholic
2. *Acheii* — Grandfather *
3. *Ashkii Ana'dlohi* — Laughing boy
4. *A-hah-la'nih* — affectionate greeting*
5. *Billigaana* — white people
6. *Ch'ihónit't* — *a spirit path flaw in art.*
7. *Chindi* — (or chinde) Spirit of the dead *
8. *Diné* — Navajo people
9. *Diné Bikeyah* — Navajo country
10. Diyin dine'é —Holy people
11. *Hataalii* — Shaman (Singer)*
12. *Hastiin* — (Hosteen) Man or Mr. *
13. *hogan* — (Hoogahn) dwelling or house
14. *Hozo* — To walk in beauty *
15. *Ma'iitsoh — Wolf*
16. *Shimásáni* — grandmother
17. Shizhé'é — Father *
18. *Tsé Bii' Ndzisgaii* — Monument Valley
19. *Yaa' eh t'eeh* — Greeting; Hello
20. *Yeenaaldiooshii* — Skinwalker; witch*
21. Yóó'a'hááskahh —One who is lost

*See Notes

R. Allen Chappell

Notes

1. *Aa'a'ii* — Long known as a trickster or "thief of little things." It is thought Magpie can speak and sometimes brings messages from the beyond.

2. *Acheii* — Grandfather. There are several words for Grandfather depending on how formal the intent and the gender of the speaker.

4. *A-hah-la'nih* — A greeting: affectionate version of Yaa' eh t'eeh, generally only used among family and close friends.

7. *Chindi* — When a person dies inside a hogan, it is said that his chindi or spirit remains there forever, causing the hogan to be abandoned. Chindi are not considered benevolent entities. For the traditional Navajo, just speaking a dead person's name may call up his chindi and cause harm to the speaker or others.

11. *Hataalii* — Generally known as a "Singer" among the Diné, these men are considered "Holy Men" and have apprenticed to older practitioners sometimes for many years—to learn the ceremonies. They make the sand paintings that are an integral part of the healing and know the many songs that must be sung in the correct order.

11. *Hastiin* — The literal translation is "man" but is often considered the word for "Mr." as well. "Hosteen" is the usual version Anglos use.

R. Allen Chappell

14. *Hozo* — For the Navajo, "hozo" (sometimes hozoji) is a general state of well-being, both physical and spiritual, that indicates a certain "state of grace," which is referred to as "walking in beauty." Illness or depression is the usual cause of "loss of hozo," which may put one out of sync with the people as a whole. There are ceremonies to restore hozo and return the ailing person to a oneness with the people.

15. *Ma'iitsoh* — The Navajo Wolf is yet another reference to one of the many forms a witch can take, something like a werewolf in this instance.

18. *Shizhé'é* — (or *Shih-chai)* There are several words for "Father," depending on the degree of formality intended and sometimes even the gender of the speaker.

20. *Yeenaaldiooshii* — These witches, as they are often referred to, are the chief source of evil or fear in traditional Navajo superstitions. They are thought to be capable of many unnatural acts, such as flying or turning themselves into werewolves and other ethereal creatures; hence the term Skinwalkers, referring to their ability to change forms or skins.

The Bible Seller

R. Allen Chappell

Made in the USA
Las Vegas, NV
07 May 2021